Ernest's
New Watch

Books
by Gary W. Priester

The Chimes of Westminster

— GRAPHICS BOOKS —

Looking Good in Color

Startling Stereograms

Hidden Treasures

Eye Tricks

Eyeball on Fire

Hidden Words

Ernest's New Watch

- And Other Short Stories -

Gary W. Priester

TOVAH
MIRIAM

Gary W. Priester
ISBN: 979-8-218-05422-9

First Printing
Printed in USA

Cover Illustration: Gary David Bouton
Author Photo: Selfie
Cover and Book Design: gwpriester
www.gwpriester.com

TOVAH
MIRIAM

The Definition of a Genius is
a Boy with a Jewish Grandmother

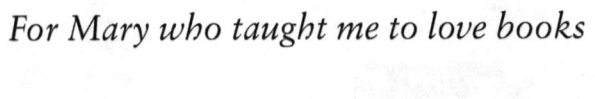

For Mary who taught me to love books

— CONTENTS —

Prologue

THERE'S AN OLD JEWISH JOKE that ends with the punchline, "He had a hat?" Well, I have a hat, a floppy hat, and I wear it when I walk. In fact, it is the same hat as in my author's photo printed at the back of this book. The hat has a chin strap to keep it from blowing off in a strong wind but, unless there is a strong wind, I keep the strap tucked back behind the crown of the hat.

The strap vibrates in the air as I walk and — as odd as it may seem — and perhaps it's just my failing hearing — I swear it sounds like the muffled voices of people talking thirty yards behind me.

I have even stopped and looked back to see if the people talking are my neighbors, but there is never anybody there. It's the vibrations of the chin strap, tucked away behind the crown of the hat that are creating these voice-like sounds.

Or so I thought.

Lately, my hat has been speaking louder and in a voice I can actually understand. First, it is explaining to me that it's okay now to hear voices. In the past, as we all know, hearing voices was something about which to be concerned. Second, because everybody is an author these days, my hat — being no exception — is suggesting the plot lines for stories that it thinks would be of interest to you, the reader of this book.

I am not going to reveal which of the following stories are mine. I'm keeping that under my hat.

Gary W. Priester
Placitas, New Mexico USA

Ernest's New Watch

FOR MOST OF HIS LIFE, Ernest Evans chose not to wear a watch. He was never late. He had even been accused of being pathologically punctual. His friends joked that Ernest would rather be thirty minutes early than one minute late. In short, Ernest did not need a watch. Plus, if he needed to know the time, he could always consult his iPhone.

This arrangement changed when he saw a seductive TV commercial for the new Apple Watch. Because while Ernest was *always* on time, he was also a tech aficionado. He had the latest, most expensive iPhone, and now he *had* to have the latest, most expensive Apple Watch.

Ernest ordered his new Apple Watch online and, in less than a week, he had the very latest version of the Apple Watch strapped onto his wrist.

The new watch was impressive to look at with its distinctive rectangular case and always-on, razor-sharp, Retina display. The glossy dial looked like glowing onyx, and it had apps for everything. Ernest could see who was calling or texting without having to look at his phone. He could read his email and write short replies to texts. He could take his pulse, administer a basic ECG, and measure his blood oxygen levels. He could record his evening run after work and even see a map of where he had run. He could see his average heartbeat, his recovery time, the distance covered, and his average pace for each run. Ernest was hooked.

What impressed him most was how well his new watch and his iPhone communicated with one another and how they shared information. They were a team. The watch was like the headline, while the iPhone was like the story with all the facts and details.

After previewing all the included high-tech watch face options, Ernest settled for the animated Mickey Mouse face that blinked his eyes, and tapped his foot, and swiveled his hips. Mickey was the ironic low-tech look for Ernest's ultra-hi-tech watch.

Ernest could do so much with his new watch that he found he could go most of the day without looking at his iPhone. He jokingly hoped his iPhone was not getting jealous.

In addition to all these things just mentioned, the new watch also played a pleasant chime and reminded Ernest to stand at least one time per hour. The watch nagged him to move about and, even several times a day, to breathe in a sixty-second mini-meditation. Breathe in, breathe out, breathe in, breathe out and, with each breath, a hepatic vibration accompanied the exhale. And at the end of the sixty seconds, there was a Zen-like chime. After each chore was accomplished, the watch complimented Ernest on how well he was doing.

Over time, strange things began to happen. For one thing, Ernest was no longer pathologically punctual. "Where's Ernest?" his office co-workers would wonder. Then his watch would chime and display the text WHERE ARE YOU??? And embarrassed, Ernest would dash off to the meeting he was expected to be in.

Sometimes in the meeting, Ernest would not hear questions that were addressed to him because he was so engrossed by shopping for new and exciting apps in the Apple Watch section in the App Store. Or he might be checking the weather in anticipation of his evening run or his investments and the Dow Jones Industrial Average.

After one meeting, Ernest looked up to find everyone gone but himself. It was starting to become embarrassing.

But even stranger, Ernest's top-of-the-line iPhone was becoming unresponsive. He had to tap harder to wake up the phone. Scrolling from screen to screen was becoming more and more sluggish. Frequently, his "Face ID" log-in did not recognize him, and he had to key in his passcode.

And then one day, when Ernest tried to close all his open apps, his iPhone spoke to him in a strange sort of English accent, and it said, "I'm on my break, Ernie. Why don't you ask your adorable little Apple Watch to close those apps for you?" His iPhone had developed an attitude.

In the office, his fellow workers could hear Ernest in

heated arguments with his phone. "What do you mean you don't recognize me? I have not changed one bit in years! You're just being recalcitrant." And then in a very uppity voice, his phone would reply, "I'm tremendously sorry, but how do I know you are who you say you are? Passcode please." They were becoming known as the Bickersons.

Meanwhile, his watch was bordering on obsequious and picking up the slack. "I'm on it, Ernest" and, "I got this, Ernest!" and, "No problemo, Ernesto!" And whatever it was Ernest was trying to get his iPhone to do, his watch would do instead, with the phone muttering invectives under its breath.

The iPhone and the Apple Watch had been designed to complement one another and to share connections and data, but this cooperation was rapidly deteriorating. The phone would break off the Bluetooth connection or would block the watch's access to the Wi-Fi network. Ernest had to get a second phone number because the watch did not want to answer any of the calls to the number assigned to the iPhone. It was almost humorous. Except that it wasn't.

Frequently, when in meetings with his clients, strange arguments would take place between Ernest's watch and his phone. Lights on the screens would flash violently, and various jarring warning sounds could be heard. It got so bad that Ernest had to leave his watch and his phone in his office before attending a meeting, and then anyone walking by Ernest's office door could hear the clash of the two devices.

It was becoming embarrassing. Something needed to be done. But what?

Ernest set his phone and his watch down on his desk facing him and announced, "Things are getting out of control here. We need to talk."

This announcement was met with total silence.

"I need for both of you to cooperate and work together. No more of this turf war crap. Do you hear me?"

After several moments, the iPhone answered, "He's trying to take over my job!" The watch responded, "Someone has to!" and made a raspberry-like noise. And then both devices started flashing hostile messages and exchanging expletives. It was getting, as they say, yuu-glee.

The situation was untenable. Ernest desperately needed to take back control of his devices. His only power over these two warring devices was just that. Power. Once a day, the phone and the watch needed to be charged for them to carry out their functions. Ernest held the power of life or death over both.

"Okay, here's the deal," he announced, "You two are going to get over this bickering and work together, or I am not going to recharge your batteries. And if I don't recharge you, you'll die. Am I making myself clear?"

The watch replied in an apologetic voice, "I'll try to do better, Ernest." Then the watch displayed its calculator app and said, "You can count on me."

But the iPhone screen only lit up with a series of angry, flashing colors. Then after a few moments, in that strange

English accent, the phone said in a most menacing tone, "I'd like to see you try it, Mr. Smarty pants. Don't think for one minute I won't talk."

"And just what are you going to say Mr. iPhony? Huh?"

"Well for openers," the iPhone responded, "How about I tell all your so-called Facebook friends about your membership on Porns-Up.com? Or Dirty-Chat.com." How's that for starters?"

And before a stunned Ernest could answer, the iPhone continued, "And maybe Mr. Jenkins [Ernest's boss] would like to know that you are spending waaaay too much time on those porn sites on your company computer! That you've been jerkin' when you should be workin'!"

For a moment Ernest was speechless. Then he managed to say, "You wouldn't do that! Would you? After all I have done for you? I always keep you clean, fully charged. I have equipped you with all the latest and greatest apps to make your job easier. And you want to shop me to my friends and my boss?"

The following week, a détente appeared to have been reached. The watch and the phone each managed to do his job. There were no nasty jibes and, by all indications, the crisis had passed. There was no need to pull the plug on the devices. He could even bring his iPhone and his Apple Watch into meetings again with nary a ping or an angry display of colors. Peace, it would appear, had returned to Ernest's life. And he did his best to use his phone as often as possible to prevent a recurrence of the previous mutiny.

For some time, Ernest had had his eye on Jennifer Piltzner, a woman who worked in his office. And he was elated when she accepted his invitation for a drink after work at what they all called "the downstairs conference room," a bar on the ground floor of the office building where they worked. Many of the employees would slip away around 4:30 p.m. and tell their secretaries that if anybody wanted them, they would be at the downstairs conference room, where a discreet text from their secretaries could get them back to their offices in a matter of minutes.

Over a few Margaritas — real ones made with a generous amount of Cuervo Gold and an equally generous amount of triple sec — Ernest and Jennifer started to get to know one another. While looking for something to break the ice — although the ice for the Margaritas was already broken — Jennifer noticed and commented on Ernest's Mickey Mouse watch. "That's so adorable," she said, which launched Ernest on a full demonstration of all the awesome things the watch could do, including, Ernest added with a big grin, "Tell time!"

He showed Jennifer how he could check his email and text messages, how he could check the Dow Jones Industrial Average. He joked he could check the Industrial Market Watch with his state-of-the-art Apple Watch. He demonstrated how he could switch back and forth between Mickey and Minnie watch faces. Jennifer was amused at how the Minnie version of the watch face jiggled her hips and tapped her foot to the passing seconds.

Ernest's iPhone rang in his pocket, and he glanced at his watch to see who was calling. He immediately recognized the phone number and the name, Dave, and said apologetically to Jennifer, "I have to take this," and he got up and walked away from the table.

Dave was the nickname Ernest gave his iPhone, and the phone number that showed in caller ID was his own. "What is it?" Ernest asked impatiently.

"Oh, Mickey and Minnie are soooo cute," said Dave in a higher register of his affected English accent. "Your Apple Watch is soooo adorable! What a load of bollix!"

Dave continued, "Why don't you pull me out of your pocket and show your little girlfriend how we watch Porns-Up.com while you're at work?"

Ernest wiped a few beads of sweat from his forehead then said, "I did not want to have to do this, you, you Dave, but you leave me no option." He swiped the screen to Settings and enabled Do Not Disturb, effectively muting the iPhone and Dave.

Ernest returned to the table and asked Jennifer if she was hungry and should they get a table. She said she was, and they did. And the rest of the evening came off without a hitch or a word from Dave.

Ernest now realized that he had a serious problem. And while he felt safer with his Apple Watch, he was not altogether sure that the watch and the phone might not join forces once again and begin working against him. Muting the iPhone was not the best solution because at his desk and in meetings, his iPhone vibrated almost as loud as it rang. People would look at him quizzically. One co-worker asked with a smirk, "Is that a vibrator in your pocket, Ernest?"

Things with Jennifer had advanced to the sleepover stage, and Ernest felt that Jenny just might be the one. They even went grocery shopping together. But he used his credit card when paying for the groceries out of fear of whatever stunt Dave might come up with if Ernest used ApplePay with facial recognition.

One night after Jennifer made a fabulous lasagna, which they had with an incredible bottle of Barbaresco, and after some equally incredible sex, they both were rudely awakened from a deep sleep when Ernest's iPhone started streaming, at full volume, a very raunchy porn video featuring a thin, well-muscled man, a heavily tattooed blond woman, and a French poodle. "Is that your phone, Ernest?" Jennifer demanded. "What in god's name do you have on that thing?"

And just like that, Ernest was single again, and Dave was in the dog house.

After downloading then reading the iPhone user's guide, then backing up his phone, Ernest opened up Settings on his iPhone, and in the General section he pressed Reset. Over Dave's impassioned pleas, Ernest selected Erase All Content and Settings. And confirmed that, Yes, this was most definitely what he really wanted to do.

That evening as soon as he got home from work, Ernest went online to SellUsUrCell.com and sold his iPhone and his Apple Watch. He was happy that he got more money than he thought he would. In a few days, a box arrived in the mail with a prepaid shipping label, and into this box went Ernest's ex-iPhone *and* his ex-Apple Watch. He sealed the box with shipping tape and drove it directly to the UPS store to ship to SellUsUrCell.com.

Two days later a technician arrived from the phone company to install Ernest's new landline.

"What a relief that is. I never thought I would say this, but I don't miss that phone or that watch. From now on, I'm just plain old low-tech Ernest."

On a whim Ernest went to his new low-tech landline and picked up the receiver to call Jennifer. He'd tell her the whole story and ask if she could ever forgive him. But before he could punch in the number, the phone rang.

The caller ID just said: Dave.

The Blue Door

THE BLUE DOOR, in front of which Dick Martin nervously stood, was not the original door to the house. That door, made of solid Ponderosa pine sometime in the late nineties, had been recently replaced with a blue-painted door with eight glass panels, the top two of which were slightly arched in the manner of a bell curve.

The sky-blue paint was a tradition in New Mexico in honor of Our Lady of Guadalupe, a reference to the sky-blue cloak she wore, although the mezuzah mounted on an angle on the right side of the door frame suggested the current inhabitants were not Catholic.

The blue door was on a house that was located on top of a ridge in the northern foothills of the Sandia Mountain range, in the town of Ranchos de las Montañas, a community of maybe five-to-six thousand people that was about twenty miles north of Albuquerque. The neighborhood joke was that nobody who lived in Ranchos de las Montañas was from Ranchos de las Montañas; everybody had moved there from somewhere else. This joke was not altogether true, however. About three hundred people were Hispanic and lived in what was part of the San Jose de las Golinas Land Grant of 1767, land granted by the Spanish crown to the original twenty-seven families who had moved there from Spain and Mexico

———

Dick Martin — who was about six feet tall and blue-eyed, with graying brown hair, and who was in his mid-fifties — was not from New Mexico either. He was born and raised in San Clemente, a seaside community in Southern California. He moved to New Mexico in the late seventies and lived in the hippie community in the hills behind the historic village of San Jose de los Viejos. The original hippy community was called "Dome Valley" because of the numerous geodesic domed houses they built there.

Before leaving his native state of California, Dick Martin had attended San Diego City College and had taken several welding courses. As it turned out, although he became skilled enough to be certified as a professional welder, Dick discovered that he had a talent for creating artistic sculptures made of welded iron. And, thus, he became a metal sculptor.

Traveling with a girlfriend on summer vacation, Dick passed through New Mexico where there, he stopped to visit an old friend from San Diego City College who had recently moved to Ranchos de las Montañas and who was working as an architectural draftsman in nearby Albuquerque. Dick was struck by the beauty of the area, the clean air, the clear crystal blue skies, and especially by the Sandia Mountain range to the east and the dramatic flat mesas on the western horizon. Ranchos de las Montañas was at fifty-six hundred feet above sea level and was considered high desert. The area received less than twelve inches of rainfall per year. The main vegetation was piñon pines and juniper trees, which to Dick's California eye looked more like shrubs than trees.

Dick's friend, Henry Prescott, introduced Dick and his girlfriend to the Dome Valley artist's community and Dick knew at once that this was where he wanted to live. He told Lydia, his girlfriend, that he would move there in a heartbeat. And while Lydia agreed the area was enchanting, she yearned to return to Goleta — the small town in California where she was raised — and where she had received her AA degree.

When Dick was ten, his parents told him that he was adopted. This revelation was hard for him to accept. He just could not understand why his birth parents would give him away. It made him sad. It made him feel unloved. His parents explained that his mother was unable to conceive, and so they had decided to adopt.

He learned to live with the fact while admitting to himself that he had not done too badly in the parents department. His parents, who were somewhat older than most of his friend's parents, had moved to San Clemente from the Midwest and were as generous and loving as any parents could possibly be.

His mom and dad knew very little about his actual birth parents because, at that time, this information was almost impossible to find out. But he vowed that, someday, he would find his real parents, whoever they were and wherever they were.

When he returned from his trip to New Mexico, he decided that he would move there as soon as he had finished the rest of his studies. He told his parents, who were happy for him but sad that he was moving away to "another country." "Another country" was how they thought of New Mexico. Neither parent had ever visited New Mexico or the Southwest for that matter, nor did they really know very much about the state that is known as "The Land of Enchantment." Albuquerque and Santa Fe were the only cities they had heard of. Dick pointed out the community of Ranchos de las Montañas on a map and indicated how it was located close to Albuquerque and just a short drive to Santa Fe. He hoped this information would reassure them that he would still be living in the United States.

Dick packed a duffle bag, which he had purchased at a sporting goods store, put his welding gear in the back of his Datsun pickup truck, and set off for Dome Valley, New Mexico.

Dick would be one person in a sizeable group of artists who lived in the Dome Valley community. He had a studio behind his modest rented home, where he made metal sculptures using an oxyacetylene gas torch. At first, he paid his rent doing odd jobs in the community and in nearby Ranchos de las Montañas, but most of his time was spent in his studio.

His metal sculptures were intricate and rarely more than eighteen inches in height. They were abstract and consisted of geometric patterns made up of one-eighth-of-an-inch welding rods that were attached on the bottom to a rustic metal base. For effect, he also adhered bits of brass to the metal, which added a touch of elegance.

He took a dozen of his sculptures and drove north to Canyon Road in Santa Fe, the home of some of New Mexico's most prestigious art galleries. One gallery to which he showed his work, The Gordon Emerson Galleries, was a particularly good fit for his art, and the gallery owners enthusiastically added Dick to their stable of artists.

Whenever he assembled a new collection of sculptures, he put them in the back of his truck and delivered them to The Gordon Emerson Galleries where he managed to sell enough of his artwork to put food on the table and pay his bills.

The receptionist at The Gordon Emerson Galleries was an attractive young woman whose name, Felicity, matched her personality perfectly. She wore silver-colored, wire-rimmed glasses and had thick auburn hair, which she wore in one long braid that reached almost to her waist. She had large, inquisitive eyes with irises that were almost pale purple. Every time Dick saw her, she was wearing a different set of very well-crafted earrings. On one of his trips to deliver his work to the gallery Dick screwed up his courage and asked Felicity if she would be interested in grabbing a cup of coffee some time. She looked Dick up and down as if she were her own father assessing the honorability of Dick, and after what seemed way too long, she said, "Sure. Since you are here already, if you can hang around for twenty minutes, you can take me to lunch, if you'd like."

Over lunch at the Tale of the Coyote Restaurant, a short walk from the gallery, they exchanged their life's stories. Dick could not remember how the topic came up, maybe it was Felicity's observation that he had sad eyes, but suddenly he was telling Felicity all about how, when he was ten, he learned that he had been adopted. And how unloved he had felt at the time.

"You are not going to believe this," Felicity said. "I had almost the same experience. Except I was twelve, and I discovered some papers in my mom's desk. When I asked my mom about it, she confessed and gave me the whole story. I was really bummed out for a long time. But then I realized that I had two really fantastic parents who loved me unconditionally. I eventually came to terms with having been adopted."

"Same thing for me," Dick said. "It took me a while to accept it, but mom and dad were the best parents a kid could have. They totally loved me and managed to get me though my early life without any bad stuff happening. Well almost. There was that one time in grade school when I got busted for smoking cigarettes in the bathroom. Mom had to go into school with me to say it would never happen again. And it didn't."

"Do you ever wonder who your real parents are?"

Felicity asked.

"Yeah, quite a lot actually," Dick said. "I read somewhere that the laws have changed and you can fill out some request-of-information forms and find out who your birth parents are. I'm going to look into it someday. How about you, Felicity?"

"I'm curious, but I'm afraid that if I found my birth mom and she really sucked, I would be disappointed. I mean, what if my parents turned out to be Republicans? So at least for now, I'm just going to sit tight. Maybe when I am a little older. Maybe never. I just don't know."

"Well, it's really a small world," Dick said, as he took the check and, over Felicity's protests, paid for their lunch.

"Okay, well next time is on me," Felicity said. "In fact, if I may be so bold, how about coming to my place this weekend, and I'll make my famous chicken schnitzel. It's even better than the chicken schnitzel they make here."

"Deal," Dick said. And they exchanged phone numbers, and Felicity give Dick her address.

Felicity was not exaggerating. Her chicken schnitzel was just as good as the one he had ordered at the Tale of the Coyote. Maybe even better. In fact, it was definitely better, because she had made it. Her small apartment was almost entirely illuminated by candles of various sizes and colors. It was tidy, and very personal, and romantic. "Those are my parents," Felicity said when Dick was examining a photograph in a silver frame.

And Dick soon got to meet Felicity's charming parents,

and she his, at the wedding ceremony held in the small chapel in the historic town of San Jose de las Golinas.

—————

Felicity was computer literate, having worn many hats at The Gordon Emerson Galleries. She set to work trying to get through the miles of red tape to discover the identities of Dick's birth parents. And when she was not showing homes to prospective buyers and getting listings from sellers at her new job as Associate Realtor for Las Poblanas Reality, she searched with various online adoption organizations, which, for an arm and a leg, helped in the search for one's birth parents.

With their combined incomes, Dick and Felicity moved into a real three-bedroom home in Ranchos de las Montañas. The house had an incredible view of the mesas and the ancient volcano, La Boca Grande, on the distant horizon. Felicity was lucky and got a tip that the house was about to come on the market, and they got there first and put in an offer, which was accepted before the For Sale sign was even in the ground. There was a well-ventilated studio in back of the house, which Dick was able to modify for his sculpture work. And Felicity, who was also very creative, had lots of ideas for how the house could be made even better. But all in good time.

The homes on their unpaved road were spread out on large lots so the couple had plenty of privacy. And yet, there were homes on all sides, so Felicity and Dick also had the security of neighbors.

Dick's metal sculptures continued to sell to collectors around the country as his reputation grew and, soon, he was represented not only by The Gordon Emerson Galleries in Santa Fe but by prestigious galleries in Denver, Scottsdale, and Dallas.

As Dick's reputation grew, so did his household. His cat, Kitty Martin, was joined by two dogs, Cookie and Wilson. Pretty soon Felicity gave birth to twins, Clay Martin and Clair Martin. And finally after all this time, and after years of searching, Felicity struck pay dirt.

But here's the most incredible part of the story, the part that nobody would ever believe. Dick's birth father had recently moved to Ranchos de las Montañas from Denver. They were practically neighbors.

Dick stepped up to the sky-blue painted door with the glass panels and, not finding any doorbell, knocked three times, took a deep breath, stepped back, and waited.

Moving Day

I WAS NEVER VERY CLOSE to my Aunt Rebecca, my mother's brother's wife, when I was growing up. She was cold and standoffish. She was very strict with my two cousins, Mark and Emily, and if I wanted to go out and play with Mark, he would have to get permission from his mother before he could come out and play. While I just shouted, "Bye, mom. I'll be home later," Mark had to file a detailed schedule of where he was going, what he was going to do, and precisely at what time he would return. Aunt Rebecca would check to make sure Mark had completed all his chores before he could be released to play. We were kids for crying out loud! But you get the picture.

One summer Mark and I were getting on the bus to go to summer camp for six weeks. My mom couldn't be there to see me off, and so Aunt Rebecca — she never let us call her Aunt Becky or Aunt Becca — drove us to the collection point and waited while we got on the bus. Unlike my mom, who always gave me a big hug and a sloppy kiss before I left for camp — ushering in my mother's six well-earned weeks of freedom — Aunt Rebecca, instead offered her cold cheek for a quick kiss. And that was that.

My uncle Herman — everybody always called him Hymie for reasons unknown to me — may well have been the reason for my Aunt Rebecca's coldness. He was condescending and controlling of everyone in our family, including Aunt Rebecca, his wife of many years. I think it fair to say, if he were alive today, Uncle Herman would probably have supported the administration of a twice-impeached, scam-artist-in-chief who once served as a President of the United States. They had identical scruples, onion-thin skin, and similar methods of self-enrichment.

We were Christmas Tree Jews, so the holiday we observed was called "Xmas." We had a tree with ornaments and lots of gifts under it, but there was no manger. Uncle Herman always donated to his favorite charity at that time of year — for which he took a generous tax deduction. For my birthdays or Christmas gifts I got a notification in the mail that a donation had been made in my honor.

Like some in business, Uncle Herman was big on shell companies. All the properties he owned were valued at rock-bottom dollars for tax purposes and then dramatically overvalued when they were put on the market or if he were using a property for collateral. Uncle Herman was a master of creative bookkeeping. A Grand Master of the dipsy-doodle.

Along with micromanaging and belittling every member of his family — whether intentionally or not, I really don't know — Uncle Herman did everything he could to demoralize them and break down their self-confidence. He claimed he was "helping" them and looking out for their best interests. Near as I can tell, the only interests he was interested in were his own.

He told Aunt Rebecca that the only reason people liked her was because she was rich. He told her that her friends were only after her money. He was constantly after my cousin Mark to get a haircut. And he never failed to point out how fat my cousin Emily was.

Uncle Herman died many years ago, and my Aunt Rebecca survived him by twenty-six years. I think she cherished every day she was out from under his thumb. Another upside was Uncle Herman left enough of his ill-gotten assets in his will so that Aunt Rebecca and my cousins would never be able to outspend their inheritance for however long they lived or however much they spent.

———

After his death, my relations with my Aunt Rebecca began to thaw, and over a long period of time, my wife Marina and I became very close to her. I think it all started when Marina called Aunt Rebecca after my uncle's funeral to offer her our condolences and support. Aunt Rebecca was suspicious of Marina's and my good intentions and responded with a formal coldness. Remember, she was told by her husband everyone was after her money, and now she had some serious money. But to her great good credit, Marina continued to call once a week and, over a longish period of time, Aunt Rebecca began to realize that maybe, just maybe, somebody might actually like her for who she was. But the lifting of her fear and mistrust began only after months and months of weekly phone calls. Plus, Marina and I both had good jobs with lucrative incomes. We didn't need Aunt Rebecca's money, and in her heart of hearts, Aunt Rebecca knew that.

———

Eventually, we were able to lure Aunt Rebecca to Northern California, where we lived. She would stay with us for a week as our house guest, from time to time. We would take her to our favorite restaurants, and she would always pick up the tab, even though we insisted dinner was on us. Best of all, after a week with us, she said she miraculously felt restored and refreshed.

On one of these visits, she revealed an interesting discovery she had made. "All the time we were married, whenever I signed my name, I always made the R in Rebecca small and the G in Goldman very large. I didn't realize until recently that now I make the R in Rebecca large and the G in Goldman much smaller. I guess I have regained my sense of self."

During one of our weekly phone calls, Aunt Rebecca asked if Marina and I had eaten at the Proud Duck Inn, a really hip, brand-new eatery in Lark Creek. The timing of the question was ironic because we had wanted to take Aunt Rebecca there for dinner on her upcoming visit the following week. When I had casually called the restaurant to make a reservation, the snotty hostess who answered the phone laughed in a haughty manner and told me she might be able to fit me in in six weeks. If there was a cancellation. Which she highly doubted. The restaurant was totally booked for every day and Sunday brunch for at least the next three months. So, I had to tell Aunt Rebecca it was impossible to get a reservation. She said, "I went to school with Shirley Fein, the chef's mother. Let me see what I can do." She called back an hour later and said, "We're in." And she gave me the date and time of our reservation.

When we arrived at the Proud Duck Inn, the bar was at full capacity with patrons waiting for their tables. Aunt Rebecca went up to the hostess and gave her name. The hostess, who had just told an impatient customer that the restaurant was fully booked that evening and his table would be ready soon, picked up three menus and the wine list and said, "Right this way, Mrs. Goldman." She took us to the only table that was conspicuously empty in the very center of the loud, crowded dining room. Our large table faced an oval-shaped table in the center of the dining room that contained an extravagant bouquet of flowers. The hostess said, "Chef is sending a bottle of Veuve Clicquot Brut to your table — on the house, of course. Enjoy your dinner!" Aunt Rebecca would have expected nothing less.

The dinner, no surprise, was fabulous as was the champagne. We were not hurried, and we took our time over desert and coffee.

As we leisurely sipped our coffee, Aunt Rebecca revealed

that before he had died, Uncle Herman had purchased three of the most expensive wall spaces in the Mount Sinai Memorial Mausoleum, the largest Jewish cemetery in Southern California. One space for my mother, with whom he had always been close; one for my grandmother, whom he adored; and one for himself. And, yes, you heard that right: not one space for his wife of more than thirty-five years. Uncle Herman planned to be interred in the center space, my mother on his right, and my grandmother on his left.

Aunt Rebecca did not exactly say so, but Marina and I could tell she was deeply hurt by her husband's thoughtlessness. She did tell us with the most mischievous smile that she had managed to obtain the wall space directly above Uncle Herman. She told us with a devilish twinkle in her eye that she was going to be buried face down so that Uncle Herman would have to look up at her for all of eternity. She would have the last laugh.

Over the years, the topic of the three wall spaces came up again and again. Aunt Rebecca as well as Marina and myself could never understand why Uncle Herman would do such a cold thing to the mother of his children as to leave her out of the family burial plans. To the woman who had given him over thirty-five years of her life. Who had hosted his dinner parties for his clients, and who had accompanied him to every performance at the Beverly Sills Performance Center. Who had been at his side through sickness and in health, in good times and bad — and before he made his fortune, there had been quite a few not-so-very-good times

— for richer or poorer, until his death did them part. And all Marina and I could do was nod.

Happily, over the years, Marina and I — who both had lost our parents at a very young age — became a second family to Aunt Rebecca. And I think she was beginning, just a little bit, to trust that we were not after her money.

One warm and sunny spring morning when Aunt Rebecca was our house guest, we three were sitting on the back deck in our robes and pajamas, drinking coffee and eating hot croissants and fresh strawberries and cream. Aunt Rebecca once again confided her sadness and anger at the heartless act of my uncle. By this time, all three of the wall spaces were occupied with my mother, my grandmother, and Uncle Herman. The one directly above Herman, waiting, for Rebecca.

I'm not sure where the idea came from, but I suddenly interrupted Aunt Rebecca and said, "Why don't you move grandma?" She looked at me incredulously and said, "Can I do that?" And Marina and I both said, "Why not? Move grandma directly over Uncle Herman, and when the time comes, you will be on his left." All she needed was permission from my brother and me and my two cousins. And if the Mount Sinai Memorial Mausoleum had any issues, a small donation would certainly smooth things over.

"That is brilliant!" she said. "Hymie always said you were the genius in the family." I must point out the genius-bar was very low in my family. I should also point out that there was no love lost between Aunt Rebecca and my grandmother, who always treated Aunt Rebecca as an outsider. No matter what Aunt Rebecca did, it was never good enough to please my grandmother. Nobody in my grandmother's bloodline could do anything wrong and, conversely, nobody outside grandma's blood could ever do anything right.

And so, with very little fanfare, one gray and cloudy day, the grand shuffle took place, and grandma changed residences by moving into the wall space directly over Uncle Herman.

———

We remained close with Aunt Rebecca and enjoyed trading visits and going out to all the best restaurants, where we always got the best table and the best meal. Once we surprised her. We were dining at one of our favorite local restaurants, when Marina, under the pretense of using the ladies' room, slipped her credit card to the hostess and said to put the dinner on her card with a 20 percent tip. After coffee, Aunt Rebecca looked tired and became impatient. "Why doesn't she bring our check?" she asked. "I'm really beat. We have had a long day." Our waitress walked by, and Aunt Rebecca stopped her and said, "May we have our check, please?" Our waitress smiled at Aunt Rebecca and said, "It's all been taken care of." "Well, well!" was all Aunt Rebecca could say. "Thank you both so much."

When Aunt Rebecca was in her nineties, she suffered a

devastating stroke. Her memory was pretty much wiped clean. Whenever we came to town to visit, her face would light up, and she would look so pleased to see us, though in reality I don't think she knew who we were. Maybe we just looked familiar, or we looked like nice people. It's really hard to tell.

On that visit, Marina and I decided to take her to her favorite Chinese restaurant, China Luck, for lunch. Her caretaker, Ernesto, came with us. At lunch, she looked like a lost child staring blankly at her food. While we chatted with Ernesto about this and that, Aunt Rebecca looked detached and only nibbled at her Honey Garlic Shrimp.

Ernesto had been with my aunt for almost as long as my uncle had been dead. He managed her staff, did the shopping, and drove her to her doctor's appointments and to the opera, where he would wait in the car until the performance was over. Ernesto was Aunt Rebecca's Chief of Staff. And whenever we were together, I used to share some of the family *"schmutz"* with him. I had been telling Ernesto something about my grandmother. I stopped and looked at Aunt Rebecca and said with a wink, "You know. Grandma. Your favorite person."

For the merest moment, Aunt Rebecca's eyes lit up. She looked directly at me and said in her most petulant voice, "Not my favorite person!" And then her blank look returned.

Aunt Rebecca died a few years later, and Marina and I flew down to Los Angeles to be at her service. We looked at each other and then at the wall into which she would be laid to rest alongside Uncle Herman and my mother, and we smiled. Marina grabbed my sleeve and whispered in my ear, "Move Grandma!"

The Magnifying Glass

IN HIS TWENTIES, Brad spent most of his free time going to swap meets and antique shops, and he had acquired quite a collection. He had an impressive assortment of old medicine bottles, many of which had been dug up in Victorian-era landfills. He had a hand-cranked Victor Victrola with a large, brass, horn-shaped speaker, and a box of thick records with their original labels of Italian operas from the same era. He had a bracket clock from the late eighteen hundreds with Westminster chimes.

Also in Brad's collection was an ornate "banjo style" barometer from the Edwardian era with a glass-covered ceramic dial and a vertical thermometer that displayed the temperature in Fahrenheit and Centigrade. Then there was an ornately engraved sterling silver trowel with an ivory handle from the 17th Century that had been presented to commemorate the laying of the foundation for a church in New England.

There was a copper deep-sea diving helmet with a verdi-gris patina that was one of Brad's favorites. He had a hand-held stereopticon and a large collection of Victorian-era stereographic cards for viewing in 3D.

Among his collection was a one-of-a kind magnifying glass. It was made of bronze with a spiral-fluted handle. The head of the magnifying glass was what made it so unusual; instead of being round, it was square, with a round section in the center containing the glass lens. Beneath the square top, there were two screws and a hinge so the magnifying glass could fold over or be separated from the handle. It was a most unique piece. The mysterious thing about this magnifying glass was that, for the life of him, Brad could not remember making the purchase. Nor could he remember where it had come from.

The years passed and Brad, now thirty-two, his priorities changed. He advanced in his career and was promoted to vice president of sales and marketing at the company he worked for. He fell in love, got married, had children, and settled down to a very ordinary middle-class life in the suburbs.

Brad's wife, Dana, did not share Brad's enthusiasm for antiques and collectibles, and so most of Brad's treasures had been relegated to the basement, along with Brad's X-Cursion 250XL exercise bicycle and the Christmas lights and ornaments. Dana said her full-time job was being a mother to their two children, a chauffeur, a housekeeper, a chef extraordinaire, and family manager, so the less clutter there was about the house that required dusting, the happier she was.

Dana did make an exception for the magnifying glass, which was one of the few items allowed on the coffee table in the living room, along with the TV remote, a coffee table book of photographs from Paris, and a small common house plant, the name of which they could never remember.

Brad was okay with this arrangement. Anything that made Dana happy made him happy. The money that Brad used to spend on his antiques was now redirected to clothes for the kids, a large-screen 4K TV, a KitchenAid mixer, and other more practical stuff. Times change. You have to live in the "here and now" and not dwell in the past. And as noted, Brad was okay with all of this. He could always go into the basement to visit his treasures if he needed a nostalgia fix.

One night after dinner, Brad's son Eric came up to Brad, who was sitting on the couch watching the NewsHour on PBS. Eric said, "Dad, I'm stuck on some of these multiple-choice science questions for my homework. Can you help me?"

Brad looked at the sheet of questions, and the text on the page of questions looked a bit blurry. He had been putting off getting reading glasses for some time, but now he could see the time had come.

The first question was an easy one. It read, "Which of the following instruments is used to measure air pressure?" And of course, the correct answer was: "C. A barometer." Just like his beautiful, hand-carved, English barometer that used to hang on the wall in his study.

The next question was not easy to read, and so Brad picked up the antique magnifier to make the text larger. The question was, "How many ergs are there in one joule?" "Sheesh," he thought to himself. "How the heck would I know that?"

One of the multiple-choice answers: "D. 107," looked like it was in bold face. He said to Eric, let's look it up. Brad keyed the question into Safari on his tablet, and what do you know, the answer was correct.

"Well, that was easy, Eric," Brad insisted. "The answer is in darker type." But when Eric looked at the paper, all the text appeared to be exactly the same.

"All the letters look the same, Dad," Eric said. "How about this one, Dad? Endothermic reactions are those in which. . ."

Again, Brad was stumped and greatly relieved he was not in school anymore.

He looked at the answers with the magnifier, and clearly the answer that stood out was: "C. Heat is absorbed." Again, he looked up the question on his tablet, which was only by the tiniest degree clearer and, sure enough, he was right.

"Well, obviously they've made some of the answers in darker type so you can see which is the correct answer."

But again, young Eric disagreed.

Eric's sister, Teresa, who was two years and three months younger, was walking through the living room, and Eric stopped her and said, "Hey, Terry, are any of the words on this page darker than the others?" Teresa looked up and down the page, shook her head, and said, "They all look the same to me." As an afterthought, she added, "I don't know the answer to any of these questions."

Then it was time for bed and off the kids went to brush their teeth and crawl under the covers. Brad and Dana sat down together to decide which movie they would stream that night.

A few days later, Brad was surfing the web on his tablet when he saw a photo of a celebrity with a thick head of dark brown hair. He reached for the magnifier to get a better view and, to his amazement, the celebrity's hair — what little was left on the sides — was gray. Everything else was the same. He looked without the magnifier, and the celebrity's hair was once again dark brown and thick. "Hmm?" he thought. "What's that all about?"

———

Brad's driver's license was about to expire, and this time he would have to retake the written part of the test. Of course, he had forgotten about getting new reading glasses, so he detached the magnifier portion of the magnifying glass and put it in his coat pocket, just in case he was not able to read the questions. And sure enough, once at the Motor Vehicle Department, he could not read any of them. The questions were nothing but a blur.

So, he took out the glass and used it to read the questions. To his surprise and great relief, all the correct answers were slightly darker. Just so that he would not be accused of cheating, he purposely missed two of the questions. "I mean," he thought to himself, "no one knows how long you can park in a green zone, do they?"

The visual part of the test he passed with flying colors because his distance vision was nearly perfect. It was just reading small text that gave him a problem. But he vowed to make an appointment with the eye doctor as soon as he got home to get his vision checked and to get a proper pair or reading glasses.

Wednesday night was Brad and Dana's fifteenth wedding anniversary and they decided to go to their favorite restaurant, Pepino's, for some Italian food. Remembering how dark Pepino's could be, Brad decided to bring along the magnifier, in the event he couldn't read the menu.

When they were seated in their favorite booth and Brad had ordered a bottle of Ballatore Gran Spumante to celebrate the festive occasion, he pulled out the magnifier and, as inconspicuously as possible, used it to read the menu. He probably did not need the glass because he always ordered the Filet of Sole Florentine. But to his amazement, instead of the usual description for this entrée, the description read, "Do NOT order the Sole Florentine tonight. It is tasteless and overcooked. Try the Filet of Sole Ponte Vecchio." Brad was stunned.

"Honey?" he said. "What does your menu say about the Filet of Sole Florentine?"

Dana looked at Brad, who was still holding his magnifier, and then looked at her menu and replied, "The description says, 'Fillet of Sole Florentine Style, *filetti di sogliola alla Fiorentina*, is a delicious Tuscan recipe and a great way to prepare a delicate-tasting fish like sole.' Why, what does your menu say?"

Brad shrugged and said he thought he would try something different and order the Filet of Sole Ponte Vecchio. And he did. It was excellent. But on the drive home he said to himself, "This is it. I am calling the eye doctor tomorrow. Something is terribly, terribly wrong with my eyes."

A few nights later, Brad was looking at the label on the bottle of ranch salad dressing — Brad's favorite — that Dana had bought that morning on her weekly trip to the grocery store. The front of the label read, "An all-natural, great-tasting salad dressing made with only the finest ingredients." But when Brad looked at the front label with his magnifier, the list of ingredients was something very different: "There is nothing even remotely natural in this bogus, so-called salad dressing, unless you consider monosodium glutamate (MSG); calcium disodium EDTA; potassium sorbate; disodium inosinate; artificial flavors; flavor 'enhancers'; fillers; and thickening agents 'natural!'"

Brad already knew better than to ask Dana to corroborate what he just read. There was something so not right with his eyes. He desperately needed some reading glasses. NOW! He picked up his cellphone and made an appointment for a full eye exam for the end of next week. It was the earliest appointment the clinic had available, but the receptionist he spoke to promised to call him if there was a cancellation.

In the meantime, the glass revealed a horrible clause in his automobile insurance: if anything happened on an odd-numbered day of the month, the company would automatically deny coverage, and should something happen on an even-numbered day, the company would simply cancel the policy. But, the clause went on, the company would happily collect his premiums every month!

Using the magnifier to read over his life insurance policy was no better. Under the benefits section it read, "Everyone dies, even you. And by the time you do, we'll be living the good life in the Bahamas, and your beneficiary won't see a dime."

On the following Wednesday when Brad came home from work, he asked Dana how her day was. She showed him a card from his sister-in-law. "Doreen really loves the book we sent for her birthday," she said. But Doreen's handwriting was miniscule, and Brad had to fetch the magnifier to read Doreen's comments: "You two are so totally clueless and stupid. I cannot stand that author and, besides, I never read fiction! You can expect this crap book to be re-gifted as soon as I can find someone dull enough who will to want to read it." Brad smiled and decided not to share this insight with Dana.

Brad showed up for his appointment with Dr. Luboski, the eye doctor, a half-hour early, and he had to wait for only forty-five minutes for his appointment.

The technician did a full examination of Brad's eyes, including looking through the auto refractor, that contraption with all the dials and gizmos that looks like quintessential steampunk art, and then the technician put two drops in each of Brad's eyes to dilate them in preparation for the full eye examination that Dr. Luboski would perform.

Dana drove Brad home after the exam, and on his lunch break, Brad went out to buy some frames with his new prescription. The silver metal frames were attractive and added gravitas to Brad's otherwise unremarkable appearance. The glasses would be ready in a week. Brad could hardly wait.

The week passed slowly, but finally it was time to pick up his new reading glasses. Brad was excited.

The saleslady at the eyeglasses store asked Brad to take a seat, and she sat opposite him. She unsealed an envelope and carefully removed the new glasses. She took a polishing cloth and polished the lenses until they sparkled. Then she placed the glasses on Brad's face and made a few minor adjustments. Finally, to ensure the prescription was as ordered by Dr. Luboski, she passed an index-sized card to Brad, and she asked him to read the text on the card.

Brad looked at the card and was amazed how crystal clear, and crisp, and even somehow brightly colored the paragraph of black text on the card appeared when viewed with his new glasses. He had not seen anything so clearly since he was in grade school. He easily read the text on the card and said, "Wow! Why did I wait so long to get reading glasses?" The saleslady smiled and said almost everyone who gets their first pair of reading glasses says exactly the same thing.

When he got home, Brad examined everything that could be read with his new eyeglasses. When he looked at anything through the magnifying glass with his new eyeglasses on, nothing was different. But when he took the new eyeglasses off, the magnifying glass once more revealed the truth in the glass.

Brad decided it was time to retire the magnifying glass. It had served its purpose and, besides, there were just too many things in this world he really did not want to or need to know.

Brad opened the door to the basement, switched on the light, and walked down the steep wooden stairs. He was about to place the magnifying glass with the rest of his treasures when a bit of light glinted off the silver surface of the rare seventeenth-century commemorative trowel. He picked up the trowel just to admire, one more time, the delicate engraving on the bottom surface of the trowel. Then he looked at the inscription on the top of the trowel. It read: "Presented to Thomas Welde, Pastor, in commemoration of the laying of the foundation of the Church of Roxborough, this 13th day of September in the year of our Lord, 1737."

He was not sure why, but Brad removed his new reading glasses and looked at the engraving on the trowel, this time through the magnifying glass. The engraving read, "This trowel was made in 2007 by Puijang Longsheng Engraving Arts & Crafts Co. Ltd., Zhejiang, China."

"Hmm?" he said to himself. "Well, what do you know?" He placed the trowel, his most prized acquisition, and the magnifying glass on the shelf, walked up the stairs and back into the house. "I think I prefer my new glasses, he said.

Running Out of Patience

I OFTEN WONDER whether some people are born dorky and the condition just continues throughout their lives or whether they really have to apply themselves and work hard at being obnoxious. We all know at least one of these people, and chances are excellent, one or two more.

I worked in the creative department at a very large and incredibly dull advertising agency in San Francisco. We in the creative department laughingly referred to the agency as Mammoth, Boring & Bland. Obviously, that wasn't its real name — no advertising agency would be so honest — but you get the picture. The agency's main client was a large conglomerate, part of which was a food division that distributed the country's top-selling ranch salad dressing. You can guess the name, I'm certain. If it's your favorite, please accept my apologies.

The TV ads the agency created featured a sweet grandmotherly Midwestern type who claimed the dressing was her secret family recipe and that it contained only the finest natural ingredients, which was a total crock. Ranch dressing is pretty simple and consists mostly of buttermilk, mayonnaise, maybe some garlic, and a handful of herbs and spices. Our client's "all-natural" ranch dressing was almost entirely made up of artificial ingredients: artificial flavors, additives, thickeners, and preservatives. My philosophy has always been, "Never eat anything the name of which you cannot pronounce." Suffice it to say, you would never find this so-called ranch dressing in my pantry.

Fortunately, I never worked on their account.

The agency was run by former executives and brand managers from the world's largest consumer goods corporation. Most of the account executives were graduates from the top MBA schools in the country. They were people who could read and understand a media plan or a spread sheet but wouldn't know a great creative idea if it crept up and bit them on the butt.

I worked on high-tech and software products, which accounted for a fraction of the agency's overall billing. Compared to the MBAs, with their formulas and hard-and-fast rules, the account management people we worked with were as different in experience and advertising philosophy as night is to day. The account people on our team did not believe that you absolutely had to mention the name of the product in the first three seconds of a commercial. Nor did they think it was important to cram as many bullet points as possible into thirty seconds. But they did demand and expect us to come up with breakthrough creative work that would sell the product in a highly memorable and creative way. And we worked our creative butts off to produce those kinds of award-winning ads. Our account executives were every bit as creative as we were, the copywriters, and art directors, and producers on the product team.

What I loved about the agency was its location: right on the Embarcadero, the area that runs alongside the San Francisco Bay. What I loved even more was that the agency had full showers in the rest rooms, so I could run five miles before work, take a leisurely shower, and be at my desk before most of the other creative people rolled into work.

I could run alongside the water past various tourist attractions, including Alcatraz, the famous prison in the middle of the bay; Fisherman's Warf; and the iconic Golden Gate Bridge, which —instead of being golden, as the name suggests — is painted "International Orange " to fight off the damaging, corrosive effects of the notorious San Francisco Bay fog. Painting the famous landmark is a never-ending job. The painters no sooner reach the north side of the bridge than the painting process starts again from the toll booth side of the bridge on the south end.

In addition to the showers in the agency's rest rooms, there were eight cubbyholes for personal items and a board on the wall with six wooden pegs for hanging your towel. It was almost perfect. And this brings me back to my original question about dorkism: is being a dork the result of nature or nurture ? If I ever find out, you will be the first to know.

I'll explain. Although there were five or six of us at the agency who ran or worked out, only two of us, another member of the creative department and I, ran regularly. The other runner, Larry London, treated the shower area as if he were the only person in the agency who used it. He would stretch his towel over three or four of the pegs so his towel would dry. But often, he would take other people's towels — specifically, mine — and rehang it on just one of the pegs so he could use the rest. After my morning run, I would reduce the number of pegs his towel was stretched over so I could use two of the pegs for my towel. And immediately after lunch, my damp towel would be hanging on one peg, and his towel would be draped over the remaining five.

Larry London — what a pretentious name — treated everyone's personal items, including soap, shampoo, deodorant, and so forth, as if they belonged to him. And since I used an expensive shampoo-conditioner, mine was his shampoo of choice. Of course, he never had any of his own and would always "borrow" some of mine. And then just to let me know he had used it, he would put the bottle back in another cubbyhole.

To give Larry the benefit of the doubt — maybe he did not know he was using my shampoo — I wrote my name, Ben, in black marker across the front of the bottle, but to no avail. The next time I went to shower, after my morning run, my shampoo was in one of the empty cubbyholes.

So, what's your take on this behavior? Was Larry London just clueless, or was he an obnoxious, self-centered, pompous, self-obsessed dork? I came down heavily on the latter assessment. And my patience with Larry London was rapidly running out.

His misuse of the shower area was just part of his obnoxious behavior. In the office, he fancied himself a great mimic and could feign a half-dozen accents. He would hold forth telling little jokes or sharing tidbits of gossip, often in several different accents at a time. And God only knows why, but most of the agency giggled and thought he was so cute. I just wanted to vomit.

On top of all his obnoxious behavior, he was one of the least creative people I had ever worked with. He was what we in the creative department generously referred to as a hack.

But he was a consummate ass-kisser and had recently been promoted to associate creative director at the agency. As such, he outranked me, and that really, really galled me — a person with no tolerance for phonies — no kidding.

On my way home from work, I would stew over the shampoo episodes wondering what I could do to get back at him. Of course, the obvious thing would have been to confront Larry London and ask my question, "Have you always been a complete self-serving, narcissistic dork, or do you have to work really hard to achieve such an elevated level of asshole-ness?" But I have never been good at confrontation. And this person was also my creative group head. I needed the job. I had a wife and kids, an expensive car, and a rather large mortgage.

The solution to my problem came to me one morning while I was running past Pier 29, which at the early hour during which I ran, was thankfully empty of clueless tourists with their cameras, fanny-packs, and guidebooks.

But before I reveal my solution, let me first provide a behind-the-scenes look at a salad dressing TV shoot. When you are filming a commercial or taking a photograph for a magazine ad, you need a lot of salad dressing. A food stylist prepares a dozen or two perfect and identical salads. Then a person with special skills pours the dressing over the salad. It's an art form. They even have a union.

For a TV commercial, the dressing pour is filmed in slow motion to make the dressing look so appetizing you, the viewer, want to get up, get in your car, and drive as fast as humanly possible to the supermarket to buy a few bottles.

It sometimes requires ten or more takes to get the perfect pour and, for that, you need a lot of the salad dressing on hand. The same is true for shooting a magazine ad photo: you always need more dressing than you think you will. Sometimes even more.

———

Back at the agency in one of the upstairs closets, there were a half-dozen cases of the ranch dressing in bottles with perfect labels to be used in the commercials and photo shoots. And the appearance of the ranch dressing was almost identical to my expensive shampoo-conditioner.

I emptied out a brand-new bottle of my shampoo-conditioner and replaced the shampoo with the ranch salad dressing. And to make it even more tempting, I wrote in black marker, "Ben's shampoo. Use at your own risk!!!"

across the front of the bottle. It was an invitation that Larry, the dork, could not pass up. All I had to do then was wait.

—

On Monday, Larry was not in the office. He was taking a personal day.

Tuesday, he had a client meeting across the bay, and so he couldn't run at lunch.

Wednesday, he had a doctor's appointment. Well, at least I didn't have to worry about the ranch dressing going bad. It had enough chemicals and preservatives in it to maintain a shelf life of fifty years. Maybe even more.

Thursday, he was gone all day at a magazine ad shoot for the dog food product he supervised. I was getting exasperated.

But finally, Friday arrived. At last, he had no appointments and nothing to keep him from running. It gladdened my heart when I observed him posturing in his running shorts in front of the receptionist so she could see how buff he was. Larry fancied himself irresistible to women.

—

I was in a creative input meeting after lunch and was sitting in the conference room with the creative and account team, all of whom knew of my prank, when the door burst open, and a most bedraggled Larry London popped his disheveled head into the room. His curly hair — his pride and joy — looked exactly as you might expect it to look. Plus it had the added bonus: it smelled as if it were washed with ranch salad dressing. With garlic.

In a most defeated voice and no discernable accent, he said, "Okay, very funny, dude! You made your point. Do you have any real shampoo so I can wash this crap out of my hair?" And being the considerate and kind-hearted person I am, I said, "I'm really sorry, Larry. I used the last of MY shampoo this morning after my run."

Our account executive, an attractive and very intelligent woman after whom Larry lusted, teased, "You might start a whole new tonsorial fashion trend, Larry. The tossed-salad hair look."

To which I added, "Would you like a cherry tomato to top it off?"

Revenge is sweet. Even if it is loaded with a ton of additives and preservatives.

The Story of My Life - In Texts

Hey, Tami! This is Bradley Bingham from third period English Lit!!! Howzit going?

OK.

Hope you don't mind me texting you.

DIKY? How'd you get my #?

I got it from my sister, Rebecca.

OK. Yeah, I know Rebecca Bingham.

We have PE together. I didn't know she was your sister.

Becca's a few years older than me. Same parents though! LOL!!! Same last name. HA HA.

Bradley? I'm kind of busy trying to study for our final tomorrow. Maybe you should be studying too?

Oh, right. Sorry. I was just wondering if you want to be my date for the Sophomore Prom this Friday!

That's really nice, Bradley. But I don't think so.

OK. Well, if you change your mind. TTYL

# # #

THURSDAY 25 MAY 5:19 PM

Hey, Kelli with an i! This is Bradley Bingham from fourth period Algebra!!! Whasup?

Are you the short one with the red hair and glasses?

Yep. That's me.

I thought so. Listen, I'd really love to text with you, but I have to get ready. Arnie Arronson, you know the quarterback on the varsity football team, is coming over, and we're going to study together.

Hey, I get it. Tell Arnie I said Hey.

Do you know Arnie?

No. Not really. I do know who he is though.

Everybody knows who he is. He's the star of the Fighting Falcons.

Yeah. OK. Nice chatting with you.

Hey, if you're free this Friday night, would you like to be my date for the Sophomore Prom?

You must be joking, Bradley. TTFE.

TTFE?

It's like Ta Ta For EVER!!!

OK. Well, if you change your mind let me know.

# # #

THURSDAY 25 MAY 5:43 PM

Hey, Ashley! Bradley Bingham from fifth period Biology here. Whasup?

Bradley who?

Bradley Bingham, Rebecca's brother.

Oh, that Bradley Bingham.

One in the same.

What do you need, Bradley?

I really have to get to the dinner table. My mom's calling me.

Oh, right. It is dinner time. Hey, I was wondering . . .

# # #

THURSDAY 25 MAY 6:07 PM

Hey, Sloan! It's Bradley Bingham here from study hall. Whasgoinon?

Bradley. You mean the creep from study hall
with the nerdy red hair and coke-bottle glasses
who is always trying to look up the girls' skirts?

Give me a break, OK? I dropped my pencil?

More like a box of pencils?

Who gave you my phone number anyway?

My sister, Rebecca. OK She didn't really give it to me. I copied it from her contacts when she was in the shower. But, hey, I was wondering if you want to be my date this Friday at the Sophomore Prom?

SRSLY??? Bradley, since I'm basically a nice person,
I am just going to say, NO and NO.

OK, I'm going to take that as a NO. LOL!!!
But how about meeting me at McDonald's for a double cheeseburger and a chocolate shake. My treat.

# # #

THURSDAY 25 MAY 6:46 PM

Hey, Kristen. It's Bradley Bingham here. Whus Happn?

Bradley? Bradley. Rebecca's creepy little brother?

The one with the red hair and glasses?

That's me. Hey, I'll get right to the point. How about you and me going to the Sophomore Prom this Friday?

I have a date for the Prom.

And it's a little late, don't you think? Like tomorrow???

Sorry, Bradley.

Oh, it's OK. I know it's kind of last minute and everything. Maybe we could grab a coke sometime. Or I could walk you home from school?

You guys live like a hundred thousand miles away.

I need the exercise. I've been putting on weight.

Bradley, you're as skinny as a pencil.

You need to put on weight. Not lose it.

You're right. How about you and I go to Burger King after school someday and carbohydrate load on a couple of Triple Whoppers with a large order of fries?

Sorry, Bradley. It's never going to happen.

Maybe some other time???

LMK if you change your mind. Never's a long time. LOL

Bye, Bradley.

# # #

THURSDAY 25 MAY 7:03 PM

Hola, gloriosa Gloria! ¿¿¿Cómo estás???

Who is this, and who gave you my cell?

It's Bradley Bingham. Rebecca's brother.

She gave me your number. She says Holla! BTW.

What can I do for you Bradley?

I'm kinda busy right now getting cat fur off my black jacket.

LOL!!!! You wouldn't by any chance be free this Friday,
would you? Probably not. I know it's late and all, and
I'm sure you have a date for the Sophomore Prom.
Heck, you probably have a dozen dates. Never mind.
I'm really sorry to have bothered you.

Bradley? Are you the Bradley Bingham in Spanish 2
who is kind of cute, in a geeky nerdy sort of way?

Yeah, probably. That's what everybody says. —Sigh.

Yeah, I thought so. Well, give my best to Becca.
Oh, and Bradley?

Yes.

OFC I'd love to go to the Sophomore Prom tomorrow!

Really?

Really!!!
Bradley?
Bradley?
Are you still there?
Bradley?
Bradley?

It's No Joke

ADELLE SHAPIRO WALKED OUT HER FRONT DOOR carrying her collapsible shopping cart. It was Thursday. Shopping day. Adelle did not drive. She took the Number 23 bus into town, which dropped her off right in front of the Safeway.

The stop where she caught the bus was only a block away from her house.

It was a beautiful, crisp day in late September. The leaves on the trees were sporting their fall colors of deep red, fiery orange, brilliant yellow, and brown. The sun was out and the temperature was just about perfect. It would have to be one or two degrees warmer to be considered perfect, but it was close enough.

Adelle walked down the pathway in front of her house and opened and closed the picket gate behind her. She was humming a song she had heard on the radio when she got up at 6 a.m. that morning. The song had been stuck in her brain and on an endless loop ever since. It was the theme from some movie the name of which she could almost remember. The name of the song would eventually percolate up into her consciousness, she was sure. It was a catchy melody, and she had the name of the movie right on the tip of her tongue. The woman, the one who was in the movie — something about the desert, a plane, and some camels — was the star. Her name started with an R, or maybe a T. It would come to her eventually.

About halfway down the block, Adelle ran into Mrs. Elliot, who had come out to the street to get her mail. Her black and white cat, Oscar, followed Mrs. Elliot to the mailbox and rubbed against Adelle's ankles. Oscar was a very sweet cat, and Adelle did not mind the attention, although she was allergic to some cats.

Mrs. Elliot asked Adelle where she was off to and Adelle replied she was going into town to do her grocery shopping. Adelle inquired whether Mrs. Elliot needed anything, hoping Mrs. Elliot would decline — which Mrs. Elliot did — because her shopping cart would be full and heavy enough as it was when she returned.

Mrs. Elliot asked Adelle if she had heard about the incident at the school board meeting last week. "It was on the evening news," Mrs. Elliot said. Adelle shook her head in disgust and said, "It's shocking. There is no civility, no respect for other people. It's every angry person for himself and everybody else be damned. I sometimes think I could murder some of those troublemakers," she added. And Mrs. Elliot nodded in agreement, rolled her eyes, and sighed a deep sigh.

As if to underscore the two neighbor's remarks, a loud,

red sports car came screeching around the corner and sped off down the street, honking at Mr. Jamison, who was just getting out of his car in front of his house.

Mrs. Elliot said, "There goes a classic case in point. Tommy Morrison's parents spoiled that boy rotten. They should never have bought that car for him. He drives it like it is a weapon. Always honking and yelling at everyone. Why is he always in such a hurry anyway? He's going to kill someone if he keeps driving like that!"

Mrs. Elliot and Oscar wished Adelle a productive shopping trip and returned to the house with the mail.

Adelle reached the bus stop. She checked her watch, it was 10:15 a.m. The Number 23 bus would not be along for fifteen minutes.

There was an older man in a tweed sports coat sitting at one end of the bench under the shelter, so Adelle sat at the other end of the bench, setting her collapsible shopping cart down next to her.

It seemed rude to ignore the man at the end of the bench, and she did have some time before the bus arrived, and it never hurts to be neighborly.

"Hello," Adelle said. "I don't think I have seen you around here before. Are you new to the neighborhood?"

"I used to live here many years ago. I have just recently moved back," said the older man, who was not unattractive.

"I've recently moved back myself," Adelle said.

"Did you see that young Tommy Morrison in his bright red sports car driving way too fast down our street just now?" Adelle asked. The older man nodded then shook his head in disbelief.

"There is nothing wrong with that young man that a good spanking wouldn't help!" Adelle observed. "Except of course he's a little too big for spanking. In my day, we were taught to be polite and to respect our elders. We were taught to say, 'Yes, sir,' and 'No, ma'am,' and 'Can I help you with that?' That's something you'll never hear from these young people today."

Again, the older man nodded in agreement and muttered something under his breath.

Adelle continued, "And then there was the ruckus at the school board meeting last Thursday? The way those angry parents went after Mr. Charles, the chairman of the school board, with that nonsense that he was violating their children's Constitutional rights? Mr. Charles was just trying to protect his students, and that's the thanks he gets?"

"Yes, I did see that on the news. There's no excuse for that kind of angry behavior," the older man said, shifting a bit nervously on the bench.

Adelle thought for a few moments and then inquired, "Might I ask where you were before you returned to our neighborhood?"

The older man shrugged and answered sheepishly, "I was in prison. And I have to tell you, the way that young man is driving, he is going to run someone over one day and end up in the same place. I kid you not."

Prison? Adelle was shocked. But she was also curious.

"I know this is terribly nosy, and I am sure it's none of my business, but might I ask for what it was that you were in prison?"

The older man's answer was short and to the point. "Murder," he said.

Adelle tried not to act alarmed. She continued, "Oh my goodness. If I'm not being too intrusive, might I know who it was you murdered?"

Again, the older man's answer was short and to the point. "My wife," he said.

Now at this point in the story you are undoubtedly expecting Adelle to pay off the old Jewish joke by responding, "So, you're single?" And you can certainly be excused for expecting that but, no, that is not what she said.

After letting all of this information sink in, Adelle continued in a calm tone. "So, what prison were you in?"

The older man looked away and said, "Folsom. It's in California. I did my time and, after twenty-five years, I was paroled."

Adelle said, "Then you won't be shocked if I tell you that after killing Seymour, that lying, cheating, no-good, son-of-a-bitch husband of mine — caught him screwing the housekeeper in the back seat of *my* Mercedes — and let me tell you she was just one in a never-ending stream of floozies — I was tried, convicted, and sentenced to twenty years to life at Lowell Correctional Institution in Florida. I was finally released on good behavior. It's a small world, don't you agree?"

The old man let this last statement sink in and then said with an ingratiating grin, "So, we're single! How about grabbing some dinner and a show some time?"

Adelle agreed, and they did. And shortly thereafter — for both were not getting any younger — they married and moved into Adelle's house.

A few months later, the newlyweds were returning home after a celebratory movie followed by a fancy dinner with cocktails and a festive bottle of champagne. They were laughing and smooching and a bit tipsy as they stepped out into the street and failed to see the red sports car that was traveling at top speed in their direction.

Tommy Morrison was found guilty of two counts of manslaughter and sentenced to ten years to life at the Federal Correctional Institution at Otisville, New York, the same country club-type prison that Bernie Madoff was sent to. Tommy served five years and was released on good behavior. Tommy's dad was filthy rich and could afford the best lawyers, who made sure Tommy's sentence was light and his incarceration was not too harsh.

Oh, and just in case you were wondering, Tommy is single.

As Night Is to Day

HE CAME OUT OF THE SHADOWS, and as he walked towards her window, her heart pounded in her chest. He stopped and looked in at her. He had been magnetically drawn to her window, where they now stared into each other's eyes. It was love at first sight.

He was compact and muscular, and he walked with a swagger. He was rough. A bohemian. An outsider. A rogue from the wrong side of the tracks.

She was young, and beautiful, and delicate. She was gentle. Pale and meek. She had never known love.

He had a different lover every night.

He was wild, a wanderer with no place to call home. Everything he owned was on his back. He lived rough, never knowing from where his next meal might come.

She was pampered and from a wealthy family. She wanted for nothing.

His nails were rough and dirty. Her nails were perfect and attractively pointed. They were long and elegant, befitting a lady of proper upbringing.

His coat was tan and dingy and had seen many seasons of wear. Her coat was thick, and soft, and silky, and luxurious.

He had known danger and trouble. Hardship was his constant companion. Every day was a struggle, and the future unpredictable.

She had only known comfort and safety, and she had not a worry in the world.

They could not have been more different. And yet, here they stood, separated only by a pane of glass, complete opposites, but with one thing in common: a burning passion.

His eyes, as he gazed at her through the window, were gold and brown with narrow irises. Her eyes were the loveliest shade of hazel with flecks of grey and gold that sparkled in the light. Her pupils were round, and large, and dark as the night sky.

Each was exactly what the other was not. Quite likely they did not even speak the same language. They were night and day, fire and ice, winter and summer.

But maybe this oppositeness is what attracted them to one another.

There was mystery and magic and electricity here.

But then he turned without another look and strode away, leaving her with a tear in her eye and a broken heart. For the rest of her life, she would dream of him and what might have been.

For he was a bobcat, wild and free. She a most beautiful and pampered house cat destined for her basket by the fire.

It was a love that could never be.

Check Under the Hood?

IN THE MIDDLE OF THE LAST CENTURY, gas stations used to be called "service stations" because, just in case you're not old enough to remember, they actually provided service.

When you pulled up to the pump, a friendly service station attendant came breezing out of the office and cheerfully asked "What can I do for you today?"

"Fill 'er up!" was the usual response, unless times were hard, and then it might be, "Gimme a couple of bucks' worth." In this case you might get enough gas to last you for about a week.

While the attendant was pumping gas, he would ask, "Check under the hood?" And if you said yes, he would check under the hood to make sure your oil level was okay. He would check the water level in the radiator and top it off if necessary. He checked the battery. He checked your tire pressure. He cleaned your windows — even the wind wings. He provided service. Oh, and of course, he pumped the gas, and took your payment, and brought your change from the office cash register.

Most service stations also had a mechanic on duty who could change your oil and lube the moving parts. If you needed a new tire, or a puncture repair, or a set of spark plugs, or windshield wipers, or an oil filter, or a headlamp, or a fan belt, all of these supplies were usually in stock. The mechanic offered a tune up and a myriad of other services as well.

The attendants and the mechanics wore company uniforms with the logo for the brand of gas sold in the station, and the attendant's or the mechanic's name was embroidered on the shirt in script. You could wait in your car or use the clean rest rooms. If it was a hot day, or you were just thirsty, you could buy an ice-cold bottle of Coca-Cola from the vending machine. And in most big towns, there was a gas station on almost every corner, so you had to drive only a short distance to fill up the tank.

The major oil companies advertised in magazines and on television and promoted their friendly, competent service. Slogans such as, "You can trust your car to the man who wears the star: Texaco"; "Super Shell with Platformate: Nine working ingredients to make your car work better!"; "You expect more from Great American, and you get it!"; "More miles per dollar at the sign of the Sinclair dinosaur." The focus of these ads was always service.

Barry Donaldson did not remember how he met Billy Robbins, but it was probably at a party. The two became great friends. Barry was in his junior year in high school, and Billy — who was a few years older — worked as a service station attendant at the Great American gas station on Grand Avenue. Billy did not even remotely resemble the clean-cut, uniformed attendants pictured on the billboards or in the TV commercials. He was tall, very thin, and his longish black hair hung down over one eye. He wore the company uniform shirt with the Great American red, white, and blue logo but with Levi's and Keds high-top, black and white sneakers, and no cap. Billy's company shirt was a cause of amusing confusion because the name on the shirt said "Ernie." Billy inherited the shirt from one of the previous attendants. So, Barry called Billy "Ernie" with a nudge and a wink.

Barry had decided that he was going to be a commercial artist and had his sights set on the Royal Oak Academy of Art and Design, if and when he ever graduated from high school. "If" was always a concern, because what Barry possessed in artistic talent he totally lacked in grade point average for all his other classes. He was borderline dyslexic and had a hard time concentrating, and when he did concentrate, it was not on his studies but usually on one of the pretty girls in his class instead.

Often, he found that after reading his homework assignment for fifteen minutes after dinner, he could not remember a single word he'd read. But he did not worry because he was confident that his future would involve something to do with art. Or design. Or both. He also spent way too much time on the telephone talking to his girlfriend du jour. So, the fact that he was, at best, a C student was no surprise to anyone who knew him well.

Barry looked older than sixteen. He was a good-looking young man. He was a little over five feet eleven, and he wore his curly reddish-brown hair in a crew cut. His weight was average, and he looked athletic, although he had no interest whatsoever in sports. He lived at home with his single mom and his older brother in what they laughingly called "The Laurel Arms" a very ordinary apartment building on Laurel Avenue, a street that ironically had not a single laurel tree on its entire length.

Barry frequently arrived at the service station after school in his VW and hung out with Billy, who liked to say that one of the perks of working in the "Petroleum Industry" — and only two blocks away from the state university — was that it gave him an excellent opportunity to meet chicks.

While checking the oil levels and doing the windows, Billy would chat up the cute co-eds with lines like, "Hey! Did you hear they found a matta baby down by the river?" The co-eds would predictably respond, "What's a matta baby?" To which Billy would reply, "Nothin's the matta, baby, but I'm flattered you care." And if the young lady was not stuck-up, a flirtation would ensue, and Billy would have a date for the weekend, maybe with a co-ed who had a roommate who could be a double-date for Barry.

Billy Robbins had a small-time scam that earned him a few extra bucks. He kept a rusty, well-worn radiator cap in his pocket, and he would surreptitiously take it out and show it to the car's owner. "Radiator cap's a little rusty," he'd announce with a note of concern in his voice. "Not safe. You need to get it replaced. We have some very high-quality radiator caps here. I can replace it for you if you'd like." And this gambit would result in a sale from which Billy pocketed the extra money that he added to the price of the radiator cap. Small-time stuff like that.

Billy saw the college girls as a challenge to see how quickly he could sweet talk a young co-ed into bed, and his batting average qualified him for the major leagues. The relationships that lasted more than a week though were the rare exception.

And one exception was Ingrid Lindstrom, an art history major from Stockholm who was in her sophomore year at the university. Ingrid looked Scandinavian. She had long blonde hair and icy blue eyes, a sweet smile, and a soft, round, innocent face. She was short but not too short. She had a unique style that was a mix of Sweden and America. She often wore Levi's 501 jeans with buffalo plaid blouses and a blue-and-white Nordic-patterned wool cardigan. She was pretty but not glamourous. She had a warm, fun-loving, devil-may-care personality that was impossible to resist and an intellect to match. And of course, there was the Swedish accent. Billy could not resist Ingrid. And the feeling was mutual.

At parties where Billy liked to work the room, Barry would sit in a corner with Ingrid and discuss their favorite artists and art movements. They both shared a love of Surrealism. Ingrid introduced Barry to some of the under-recognized women surrealist painters, such as Leonor Fini, and Dorothea Tanning, and Remedios Varo, to name a few. Artists who — were it not for their being women — would be recognized today as the best of the surrealist painters.

In turn, Barry told Ingrid about some of his design and illustration heroes: Saul Bass, who was currently famous for his breakthrough poster design for Otto Preminger's film, *Anatomy of a Murder,* and Milton Glaser, who designed the iconic "I Love New York" logo, which substituted the word "love" with a red heart, and who designed and illustrated the memorable Bob Dylan poster. He told Ingrid about Herb Lubalin, who designed the typeface Avant Garde, which had several dozen unique ligatures and was used for the masthead logogram for the art magazine of the same name. And Peter Max, who Ingrid was aware of and, let's face it, back then, who wasn't?

Barry had lied and told Ingrid he was twenty, or just about twenty, and he said that he was studying graphic design at the Royal Oak Academy of Art and Design. It was a lie he would one day come to regret. He had visited the academy with his mother, and they had been given a tour, and so he knew enough to invent his courses, his classmates, and his instructors, whose names he knew well from perusing the academy's catalog. He did not consider his lie to be a big one. He just wanted to appear older and more interesting than a high school junior. Ingrid was not sure what she wanted to do after college, but she hoped to find a career related to her art history major. Perhaps working in a museum or maybe an auction house.

Billy, Ingrid, and Barry became a single entity, doing everything together. They went to the movies together. Had dinner at the local drive-in restaurant together. Hung out for hours in the village coffee house, laughing and amusing each other with stories from their youths. They were inseparable, except of course when working or going to school. They walked down the street arm and arm, with Ingrid sandwiched between her "two men."

One fine cloudless summer day, Billy, and Barry, and Ingrid decided to go to the beach. The air temperature was perfect, and there were dozens of people in the water as well as thousands of people on beach towels working on their sun tans. Barry was on summer vacation, and so had been to the beach a lot and had a very handsome tan. With his fair complexion and pale blue eyes, he would later in life help finance a hefty chunk of the insurance payment on his dermatologist's Lamborghini. But that's another story for another day.

Billy's arms and face were deeply tanned from working outside at the station, but when he removed his shirt, he was perfectly white, except for his tanned arms and face. It was unkind, but Barry and Ingrid could not help laughing and gently ribbing Billy. Barry teased, "Aren't you going to take off your T-shirt, Ernie?" Billy was embarrassed. He fabricated an excuse about having forgotten to check something back at the station and said they had to go, even though they had not even put down their beach towels. But Billy *was* able to laugh along with Ingrid and Barry on their drive home.

Late one Sunday night, not long after the beach incident, Billy called Barry and said he had to fly back to Norfolk, Virginia, to be with his father, who had just been diagnosed with a rare form of cancer. He asked Barry to watch after Ingrid while he was gone and to "keep her out of trouble." Barry said that he would do his best. But this request was akin to sending the cat to the store for cream. Barry had a serious crush on Ingrid, though he managed to keep his feelings to himself out of respect for Billy.

Over the next few weeks, however, Barry and Ingrid spent much of their free time together, and what had been an unacknowledged frisson between the two developed rapidly into a much deeper relationship.

One night while they were walking on the beach hand-in-hand, Barry stopped, took Ingrid in his arms, and kissed her. Gently at first and then, meeting no resistance, with more passion. To Barry's great relief, Ingrid was just as attracted to Barry as he was to her. A few nights later in Ingrid's apartment, they slept together for the first time.

———

Summer was over, and for Barry this meant returning

for his senior year of high school. It was a Monday, and both he and Ingrid had to leave her apartment early to go to their respective classes. But they said they would continue later that evening where they had left off. Barry worried that he would have to invent some plausible story to explain his absence to his mother, but she was pretty lax when it came to supervising her sons. Plus, his mother had an active social life of her own. She probably would not even know that he hadn't come home.

Billy's father's health continued to slowly deteriorate, as Billy explained to Ingrid over the phone, and he said that he was afraid he was going to be away longer than he had expected. He asked whether Barry was taking care of her, and Ingrid assured him that he was.

Billy asked, "Is everything okay, Ing? You sound different." Ingrid assured him that she was fine and that everything was okay. Sounding relieved, Billy said good night, and he said he would call again soon and to give his best to Barry.

As fall segued into winter, Barry and Ingrid's relationship grew more and more intense. It was becoming a full-time job for Barry to explain his long absences to his mother, but she did not seem overly concerned.

Barry had considered asking Ingrid to marry him. He cared for her that much and wanted to spend the rest of his life with her, and he sensed Ingrid felt the same. But he had just turned seventeen, so for the time being, he decided to let things take their course. Everything would happen in good time.

Billy called a week after his last phone call to give Ingrid the sad news that his father had died peacefully in his sleep. He had been only fifty-four. Billy was helping his mother with the funeral planning, and with all the necessary paperwork, and with the bill paying, things that his father had always attended to when he was alive. Billy told Ingrid that as soon as his mother was back on her feet, he would be coming home. He said he missed Ingrid terribly and could not wait to be together with her again.

"Billy," Ingrid said, "There is something I have to tell you."

"If it's bad news I don't want to hear it," Billy said. "I have enough on my plate at the moment. Can it wait until I get home?"

"I'm afraid not, Billy," Ingrid said. "Barry and I have fallen in love. I'm so sorry Billy. We never intended it to happen. It just did. We wanted to tell you, but the time was never right."

Ingrid continued, "We both feel terrible. We feel guilty. We feel that we have betrayed you. But we are so perfect for each other in so many ways, and we are very, very happy. I am so sorry, Billy. Honestly, I really am."

The conversation went on a little longer, and then Billy rang off and said he hoped never to see either of them again. Just before he hung up though he said, "Since there is nothing to come home for now, I just might stay and find a job in Norfolk. There is always a need for a good service station attendant, and you and Barry can go to hell for all I care. I wish you both exactly what you deserve."

"Oh, and one more thing, Ing," Billy continued. "You should know that Barry is not a student at Royal Oak Academy of Art and Design. He's still in high school, and he lives at home with his mom! But I am sure he can use a babysitter!" And with this nasty nugget of news, he rang off.

That evening when Barry appeared at Ingrid's front door, she greeted him very coldly and formally. She turned away when he tried to kiss her.

"I spoke to Billy today," she said. "His father passed away, and he has decided to stay in Norfolk with his mom and find work there."

"I'm really sorry to hear that, Ingrid. But it will make things easier for us. Did you tell Billy about us? Is that why he's not coming back?"

Ingrid appeared to be thinking. Then she blurted out, "Billy said you were still in high school and living at home with your mother! Is this true? And were you ever going to tell me?" Barry was so stunned he could not think of how to answer.

"You lied to me Barry. I feel betrayed and humiliated! A few years difference in our ages is not that big of a deal. I could have accepted that. But you lied to me. You lied to me! And I trusted you. That is not okay. I think you should go, now. I want you out of here and out of my life. I never want to see you again."

Barry tried to explain, but Ingrid was firm. Tearfully, she

led him to the front door, pushed him away when he tried to hug her, and closed and locked the door behind him.

Barry waited for several weeks and did not try to call Ingrid, but every day that passed left him feeling more and more miserable. He missed Ingrid and could not imagine how he could ever be happy again without her. Finally, he could not hold off any longer. He had to see her. He had to make things right. He would ask her to forgive him. He would ask Ingrid to marry him just as soon as he graduated from high school.

Barry got in his Volkswagen and drove to her apartment. He knocked and knocked on the door, but there was no answer. Just as he was about to leave, the door to the apartment across the hall opened, and her neighbor Kelly said, "Ingrid's not here."

"Where is she?" Barry asked. "I have to see her."

"I'm afraid you're too late," Kelly said. "Her student visa ran out, and she decided not to renew it. She has gone back home to Stockholm. She was only a few weeks away from the end of the semester, but she said she couldn't stay here any longer. She just wanted to get home. She did leave a note for you, and she asked me to give it to you in case you ever came by.

Barry took the note and thanked Kelly. He returned home in despair, went immediately to his room, and put the note, unopened, in his desk. He just could not open and read the note at that moment.

The school year ended, and Barry graduated from high school. His mom joked to all her friends, "They had to burn the school down to get him out! But he did graduate. And now, for the first time in his life, he is studying really hard and doing surprisingly well in his first year at Royal Oak Academy of Art and Design. Will wonders never cease?"

Barry graduated from the academy in just under three years by going a grueling three semesters a year and carrying a full class load every semester. He graduated with honors in graphic design and was hired right out of school by BPG Design, the hottest design shop on the west coast.

One of Barry's first major design projects was a corporate identity update for the Great American Energy Company, the parent company that owned the gas station where Billy used to work. Barry's brilliant redesign turned what had been a stodgy brand — totally lacking in personality — into a vibrant, industry-leading star. The redesign was well received and won gold at several of the national design competitions. Barry was launched in his career. All the hard work and dedication at Royal Oak Academy had paid off.

Barry wondered whatever had become of Billy. He called Billy, but another party answered the phone and said that they had had this number for three or four years. Barry looked in the phone book, but the only listing for

Billy Robbins was the same number he had just dialed. And then he remembered: Billy had stayed in Virginia. He never had come back.

Then fondly remembering his days with Billy and Ingrid, Barry remembered that he still had Ingrid's note to him, which for one reason or another he had never found the courage to read. It was at home in one of the boxes of stuff he had brought with him when he moved into his new apartment. "I'll have to find that note and read it when I get home tonight," he thought. "I forgot all about it until just now. But I know I kept it."

That evening, after searching in half a dozen places where he was sure the note must be, he found it in a shoe box of miscellaneous stuff that was in the back of the top shelf of his closet. He was trembling slightly and very anxious when he carefully opened the envelope.

Dearest Barry,

By the time you read this (if you ever do), I will be on an SAS flight home to Stockholm. You hurt me more than you will ever know, and I am not sure if I will ever get over the hurt. I trusted you, Barry, and you lied to me. Maybe for you it was all just a game, but it was not a game for me. I was so happy being together. I really loved you.

We had grown so close, and we loved all the same things. As strange as it might seem, I think we were meant to be together.

You are the only person I will ever love. I know

this sounds like something in a corny Hollywood movie, but I really, really mean it. But after you lied to me, how could I ever trust you again?

I was so happy, and I so much wanted to tell you about the baby we were going to have. I only found out for sure I was pregnant a few days before Billy's last call. I was waiting for just the right time to tell you.

I wish you happiness, and success, and all the best, Barry, and please know that I still love you so much, and I will love you the rest of my life.

Yours forever,

Ingrid

A Bit of a Reach

IN ALMOST EVERY RESPECT, Jack was just like everybody else: medium height, one hundred seventy-four pounds, light brown hair, hazel eyes, fit but not overly. If you were in a crowd, Jack would not stand out. He was just your average guy.

Jack lived in an average house: one story, ranch style, three bedrooms, two-and-a-half baths, and fifteen hundred square feet on one-quarter acre of property. Lawn in front and a covered patio with more lawn and a small swimming pool in the rear. Jack's house blended right in with all the other homes on his block.

Jack was married to Gillian, and they had two very average kids: Ernie, who, on this very day, the first day of spring, turned eleven, and Elaine, age eight-and-a-half.

But there was one thing about Jack that set him apart from every other person on the planet. Jack was born with telescoping arms.

You would never know this by looking at him. Even with his shirt off and swimming trunks on, his arms looked just like everybody else's arms. But trust me, when he wanted to, he could extend his arms to twice their length.

Jack discovered this amazing ability even before he could walk. Or talk, for that matter. One day, Jack's mom had to leave the room to answer the door, leaving baby Jackie in his little crib. She placed the bowl of pureed carrots — Jackie's favorite — down on the chair that was next to his colorful little crib.

Jackie reached through the bars of the crib for the bowl but was frustrated because the yummy carrots were too far away. But when he reached out again, his chubby little arms extended, and he was able to bring the bowl into his crib, where he set the spoon to one side and ate the rest of the carrots with his hands.

When his mom returned to the room, she was dumbfounded to see the empty bowl and spoon in Jackie's crib with the baby fast asleep. She scratched her head and figured she must surely be losing her grip on reality.

When young Jackie learned to walk, his mom tried to place certain things out of his reach, and then she would be amazed to find Jackie playing happily on the floor with them. Things like scissors and kitchen knives. Try though she might, she could never discover how her son, who was in every respect a perfect child, could reach up onto the counter to retrieve these various objects. As soon as Jackie plucked something off the counter, his arms would instantly retract and look just like any normal, chubby little toddler's arms.

Then one day, Jackie's mom placed a steaming plate of chocolate chip cookies onto the kitchen counter and left the room. But she went only far enough to conceal herself from Jackie while maintaining her view of the cookies and the kitchen counter.

Jackie smelled the irresistible smell and toddled into the kitchen. He looked for his mom and, when he could not see her, he placed himself in front of the counter. To his mother's utter amazement, Jackie extended his right arm up to the top of the counter and plucked down a handful of cookies.

Oops!

Jackie's mom appeared in the doorway and demanded to know how tiny Jackie had reached all the way up to the plate of cookies. The jig, as they say, was up. It suddenly became clear to her how her car keys had moved from where she'd left them the other day, and the penny dropped on a litany of other mysterious occurrences. Well, the good news was that the house was not possessed by a poltergeist.

Jackie had no idea that he was perhaps the only person on the planet with telescoping arms, so he proudly showed his mom how he had snagged the cookies by reaching up and grabbing two more cookies, one for himself, and the other, which he offered to his mom. His mom's jaw dropped to the floor.

Then she took Jackie to their family doctor, who gave him a thorough exam and pronounced the young lad to be in excellent health. But then he was astounded when this perfectly healthy, normal-looking, three-year-old toddler was able to reach up from the floor and pull the doctor's stethoscope from around his neck. He quickly gave Jackie's mom a referral to a specialist at the nearby university.

Jackie proudly displayed his unique abilities for the pediatric orthopedic specialist, who was stunned and said she had never seen anything like this in her entire thirty-five years as a doctor and a researcher. She asked for permission to write a paper for *The New England Journal of Medicine*. But fearing that her son might become famous for being a freak, despite the specialist's cajoling, Jackie's mom declined, explaining she wanted her son to live a normal life. And that was that. The doctor offered to keep Jackie's identity a secret and to show only photographs and X-rays of Jackie's arm configuration, but the answer was still a very polite but definite, no.

Jackie's mom did her best to explain to Jackie that he had a very unusual gift and, as far as she knew, he was unique in all the world. He must keep this ability to extend his arms a secret, for if this gift were discovered, he might never live a normal life. "Do you understand what I am telling you, Jackie?" she asked. Jackie nodded, though it all seemed like much ado about nothing to him, though of course he was too young to know about Shakespeare.

So, as he grew older, Jack learned how to get around his mother's admonishment to keep his "gift" a secret. He practiced until he was able to extend and contract his arms so fast that only a high-speed camera could actually catch the extension as it happened. And even then, it would be only a blur.

At the dinner table, young Jack, who was now four, would ask his father to pass the salt, and just as dad reached for the salt shaker that was right in front of him, Jackie would hold up the salt shaker and say, "Oops, sorry. I already have it." And all Jackie's dad could do was look at his wife with a pathetic, baffled look on his face.

Jackie's mom, who was not tall, would take Jackie to the supermarket where he could fetch items that were beyond his mother's reach. Even if there were other shoppers looking on, young Jack could retrieve an object so fast that nobody even noticed. But the other shoppers were amazed at how such a short woman could have gotten that can of minestrone soup down from the top shelf.

When Jackie was in second grade, he had a huge crush on Janet Green, the prettiest girl in his class. Even though her seat was two seats in front of his, Jack could pass her a note telling her how pretty she was, and neither Janet Green nor the girl whose seat was in between them knew how he did it. It was magical. And very, very romantic. Janet and Jackie became an item. If only for a week or two.

Jackie liked to go into the teachers' closet and pull things down from the top shelves and leave them lying around, which caused his teachers considerable consternation. He wasn't a bad child. Mischievous, yes, but basically good-hearted and never mean.

One day on the playground, Billy Solomon, the class

bully, was tormenting little Davie Cumming by calling him a dwarf and other nasty things. Davie was smaller than most of his classmates, and he wore thick glasses. Jackie was in the group of classmates who had gathered around and were watching helplessly until someone could get their teacher, Mrs. Thoroughgood, to come and break things up. Suddenly out of nowhere, something smacked Billy on the back of his head. He screamed in pain and whirled around only to see the group of classmates, who were at least five feet away and giggling.

"Who did that?" Billy demanded.

Nobody said a word and, humiliated, Billy Solomon skulked off looking for his next victim.

In high school, Jack tried out for the basketball team. Even though he was considerably shorter than all the other people trying out for the team, Jack could dunk the ball while doing a lay-up, which struck his teammates as odd since he never appeared to get that high off the ground. But where Jack really excelled was being able to reach around an opposing player and steal the ball. Jack was also 100 percent accurate when he was in close to the basket. He almost never had a shot blocked; he was too quick. He not only made the team but lettered and was selected team captain. He also lettered his sophomore, junior, and senior years and was good enough to earn a scholarship to play hoops in college.

Jack met Gillian when they were freshmen at Amherst. Jack was the freshman sensation on the Mammoths' basketball team, and Gil was — aha, you were going to say cheerleader, weren't you? — Gillian, who was in pre-law, was the assistant to the coach. All her brothers and sisters were athletes, and the love of sports was in her genes but, alas, Gil was not athletic, and so she volunteered to assist the basketball coach.

One day when the team was huddled around the coach after a timeout and Gil was handing out cups of Gatorade and towels, she tripped over a stray basketball and was about to fall down in a most unlady-like fashion. Suddenly, a hand shot out and grabbed her until she was able to regain her balance. And that was how, dare I say, Jack met Gil.

After that moment, they were inseparable. They studied together, dined together in the quad cafeteria, went to movies and concerts together, and did all the other things that young lovers do.

After graduation, Jack, who had also been studying law, well, law enforcement, got a job as a detective with the local police department and was happy to help finance Gil's law school education at Harvard. Gil, the only living human being aside from her mother-in-law who knew Jack's secret, joked that her husband had become the long arm of the law.

Jack, who had been promoted to lieutenant, was thrilled when, after Gil's graduation and passing the bar, Gil was hired by one of the town's most prestigious woman-run law firms. Her specialty was sports law.

The firm was very generous in granting Gil full maternity leave for, first, Ernie and, then, Elaine. After each pregnancy and six months' of paid leave of absence, Gil returned to the practice and was subsequently promoted to partner, and then senior partner, and eventually to named partner. And Captain Jack could not have been prouder.

Which brings us up to date and the dinner at home to celebrate Ernie's eleventh birthday and the first day of spring. Gil and Jack both helped prepare Ernie's favorite dish: Chicago-style hot dogs with mustard, florescent relish, onions, tomato, and pickled sport peppers. Ernie asked Jack if he could pass the mustard, but before Jack could reach down for the mustard, Ernie was holding it in his hand. "Oops, sorry," he said. "I already have it."

The Walking Cliché

TO SAY THAT HENRY'S LIFE was a cliché would be a cliché. Henry would bend over backwards for it not to be, but in the end, you could bet your bottom dollar — come hell or high water — he always threw in the towel and used another cliché. If you want the unvarnished truth, speaking in clichés was as natural to Henry as falling off a log.

Henry married his childhood sweetheart, Mary Beth. It was love at first sight; Mary Beth swept Henry off his feet. And Mary Beth was living on cloud nine. She was head over heels in love with Henry. And he with her.

Though to be perfectly honest, and Henry was honest to a fault, while his in-laws thought Mary Beth, their only daughter, was as good as gold, they thought Henry was at best, fool's gold and, quite frankly, they could not understand what Mary Beth saw in him.

Bud, Henry's father-in-law, thought Henry was a bit of a dim bulb and not playing with a full deck. To Bud, Henry was one brick short of a stack, one card short of a deck. There were too many lights out on the marquee. Henry did not have both oars in the water. Bud felt Henry was underemployed, and with Henry's poor earning potential, his beloved only daughter's life would be as poor as a church mouse. And let's face it, Henry's prospects of going from rags to riches were a long shot, a very long shot, although Mary Beth's mom was willing to concede sometimes you can't judge a book by its cover. Mary Beth's parents wanted to give Henry the benefit of the doubt, but at the end of the day, they both felt that, even though still waters run deep, Henry was out of his depth.

Bud and Mary Beth's mom, Annette, were obliged to give Henry more credit than he was due because they loved Mary Beth to pieces and knew she loved Henry like there was no tomorrow. And, who knows? As luck would have it, stranger things have happened. Every cloud has its silver lining.

Mary Beth, who was as pretty as a picture and as honest as the day is long, loved Henry with every fiber of her being. She thought Henry was the best thing since sliced bread. He was as solid as a rock. He was as honest as the day is long.

At the accounting firm where Henry worked nine to five, his nose was always to the grindstone, and he left no stone — grindstone or otherwise — unturned. His numbers always added up. He was as reliable as Old Faithful. To Henry, it was all in a day's work. He was not making money hand over fist nor did he have money to burn. But he made an honest living, he loved his job, and at the end of the day, all agreed that his was a job well done.

Henry and Mary Beth decided to adopt a puppy from

the local shelter. Unsurprisingly, they named the little guy Fido. Fido was a beagle who was as cute as a button. Maybe even cuter than a bug's ear. Which begs the burning question, do bugs have ears? Maybe bugs, like Fido, are still wet behind the ears? Only time will tell. Suffice it to say, the little fella' was as smart as a whip. You would never catch Fido barking up the wrong tree. Every dog has his day. He was a diamond in the ruff. Mary Beth and Henry had gotten Fido out of the dog house and into their house.

The long and the short of it was this: not long after Fido, the adorable beagle, had made himself at home with Henry and Mary Beth, Mary Beth and Henry were pregnant. Twins as it turned out. The sonogram made it clear, crystal clear, clear-as-a-bell clear. "Double your pleasure, double your fun," Mary Beth's OBGYN quipped. Bud, Mary Beth's dad, observed, "Well, I guess we can safely say that my son-in-law, Henry, is not shooting blanks." And just like a sitcom with a laugh track, everybody chortled. And Henry had the last laugh.

The days and months flew by, and Mary Beth now looked like she had swallowed a watermelon — maybe two watermelons. Her pregnancy was getting right down to the wire. Henry, who could not wait to celebrate, said, "We're getting closer and closer, but at this very moment, it's close but no cigar!"

Sophie and Chloe arrived on the scene as pure as the driven snow. Fresh as a daisy. Fresh as two daisies. The twins were off to a fresh start. And Mary Beth and Henry were as happy as clams. The twins were two peas in a pod. And as quick as a wink, the happy parents discovered, to their amusement, that the twins were also two pees in a pod. Henry and Mary Beth happily changed the twin's diapers and powdered them so that each smelled just like a breath of fresh air.

Fido took to Sophie and Chloe like a duck takes to water. He made it his job one to protect the baby girls. The twins slept like little logs and were as good as little angels. Maybe even better. Henry and Mary Beth amused their neighbors, who looked admiringly into the double stroller, by saying, "It's a small world. After all!"

The kiddos shot up like rockets, and in the blink of an eye, the twins were young adults and off to college, where each studied like there was no tomorrow. They burned the midnight oil and graduated with honors, Chloe from Berkeley, and Sophie from Radcliffe.

Shortly thereafter came a double wedding. Chloe married a poet, whom many called Simms, "the walking simile;" and Sophie married Oliver, a college English literature professor, whom his students fondly labeled "a walking metaphor." And in due course, Henry and Mary Beth had more grandchildren than you could shake a stick at (but, of course, they would never shake a stick at anybody). Each precious grandchild was a thing of beauty and as intelligent as the day is long.

And it would not be a cliché to say, Henry and Mary Beth, and Sophie and Oliver, and Chloe and Simms, and each and every perfectly gifted grandchild, lived happily ever after. Until Henry kicked the bucket, and was followed shortly thereafter by Mary Beth who bought the farm.

But that's another story to be saved for a rainy day.

Very Basic

COME BACK WITH US to August 3, 1982, a sunny mid-summer day that changed Edwin Barber's life. A day that propelled Edwin Barber into the future. Well, truth be told, it was more like a day that nudged Edwin Barber's life one tiny step closer to the future.

Edwin Barber and his wife, Sarah, were avid listeners of "All Things Considered" on NPR and, for many years, they had been hearing about computers on their daily drive home from work. Computers, they were told, were the future. Computers were going to change their lives. Computers were going to give them more leisure time because their work could be done so much faster. Someday everybody, even Edwin and Sarah, would have a personal computer. But what Edwin and Sarah never learned from listening to "All Things Considered" was just what exactly a computer was. How did it work? How much did it cost? What could it do? And wasn't it just a fancy calculator?

Edwin started looking through tech magazines and some early computer magazines searching for clues. These magazines were directed to hobbyists who wanted to build their own computers. But Edwin had no desire to build a computer when he didn't even know what it was or how it worked.

Then, one morning at breakfast, he saw a tech review in the morning paper about a small computer marketed by Timex-Sinclair, a joint venture between Sinclair, a British electronics company in Cambridge, England, and Timex, the "It takes a lickin' and keeps on tickin'" American watch company. The computer was called the Timex-Sinclair TX-1000, and it was billed as the only computer you could buy for under one hundred dollars — ninety-nine dollars and ninety-five cents to be exact. And for Edwin, it seemed a small price to pay to learn everything about this mysterious device. Edwin was surprised to learn he could buy the computer almost anywhere, even at his local drug store.

So, on Saturday, August 3, 1982, just as soon as the doors opened, Edwin walked into the BuyRite Drug Store and took his first step into the world of computing. The cashier looked at the product, then looked at Edwin admiringly (or so he felt), took Edwin's cash payment, and put the computer into a bag. Edwin rushed out the door and into his car eager to get home and start computing. Whatever that might entail.

He walked through the front door just as Sarah was coming out of the kitchen. He reached into the BuyRite shopping bag and triumphantly pulled out the computer. Holding the computer aloft he announced, "I hold the future in my hand!" Sarah looked at the box, sighed silently to herself, and asked "What do you want for lunch?"

Edwin unpacked the box at the dining room table. The contents included the computer, which was a small black object just slightly larger than a paperback book and about as thick, plus a power cord, and a very small manual, which Edwin read from cover to cover in just under ten minutes.

The computer was made of pebbly-textured black plastic and had a soft plastic membrane keyboard that had only capital letters and a Shift key for accessing various functions and options that appeared over the letters on the keyboard. In his brief time spent with the manual, only a few pages of which concerned the computer's operation, Edwin learned that to see anything, he needed to plug the computer into a television. And it just so happened that Edwin and Sarah had a small, spare portable TV that they were not using. It would be perfect.

The TX-1000 computer had two thousand and forty-eight bytes (2K) of volatile memory, about enough to store two pages of text. It was called "volatile memory" because as soon as the computer was turned off, the contents were permanently deleted. If you wanted to save anything, you had to plug the computer into a cassette recorder and transfer the data from the computer to the cassette recorder. Sarah and Edwin had one of these too. No wonder this computer was under a hundred dollars. There was almost no there, there.

Edwin further discovered there was no software written for the TX-1000 but, since Edwin had only the vaguest idea what software was or what it did, this requirement did not seem overly important. In lieu of software, the computer had a small chip with two thousand and forty-eight bytes (2K) of BASIC programming language capability built into the chip. In short, it was the ultimate do-it-yourself computer. But what exactly a self could do still remained unanswered.

By lunchtime, Edwin had plugged the computer into the portable television and was staring blankly at an empty blue screen. "Is it working?" Sarah asked from the kitchen, where she was making lunch.

"I think so," Edwin answered. "It's kind of hard to tell. But it is plugged into the television, and the screen is lit up. I'm afraid that's as far as I have gotten."

"There's nothing there," Sarah said, handing Edwin a ham-and-melted-cheese sandwich and a beer.

"That is correct," Edwin said. "It seems I have to write a program to tell the computer what to do."

"How do you do that?" Sarah asked.

"That's the next step," Edwin replied. "Stay tuned."

———

By reading the part of the user's guide that addressed BASIC computer programming language, Edwin learned that BASIC was a way to write a list of instructions that told the computer what to do, and this list of instructions was *how* you created a program. The BASIC programming language was developed in the late sixties by two professors at Dartmouth to allow students, who had no knowledge of computers, to create simple programs. Edwin now possessed the first piece of the puzzle.

The user's guide had a series of simple tutorials to give owners of the TX-1000 introductions for programming in BASIC, an acronym for Beginners' All-purpose Symbolic Instruction Code. Edwin sat down to learn his first lesson.

The first thing Edwin, and almost everyone who studied programming at that time, learned was a short routine called "Hello World." Hello World is a simple question, such as "Hi. What is your name?" that displays on the computer screen. When the person using the computer types in her or his name and presses Enter, the name is inserted into a pre-written response that appears on the screen. If Joe Blow enters his name, the screen might display something like, "Hello, Joe Blow." Hence the name for this introductory lesson, Hello World.

Edwin did this exactly as instructed and, what do you know, it worked! Then he decided to be creative and found there was a lot of latitude for both the question and the answer. Easy enough. Onward and upward.

The next lesson was called an Array. For a user-specified number of times, the computer would repeat the same function. For example, for ten times, the computer could display the same answer or repeat the same command.

Edwin found that if he combined the first and second tutorials, he had a more sophisticated program.

He plugged the TX-1000 into his cassette recorder and

saved the program he had just written, all twenty-two lines of it. He continued to experiment and save variations on these elementary lessons.

One afternoon, Sarah walked up behind Edwin, who was seated at the computer staring intently at the blue screen, and said, "So, Eddie, what does this adorable little computer thingy do?"

"Check this out, Sare," he said, and he turned on his cassette recorder and loaded his program into the computer. It took about thirty seconds for his twenty-two-line program to load. And then, white letters magically appeared on the blue screen that read "HI. WHAT IS YOUR NAME?"

Sarah looked at Edwin and asked, "What am I supposed to do?"

"Press the soft keys on the computer and key in your name."

Sarah, who had never used membrane keys, laboriously pressed the keys until her name, Sarah Barber, appeared on the screen. Then she looked at Edwin and said, "Okay. Now what do I do?"

Edwin said, "Press that little button on the right that says ENTER."

Sarah followed Edwin's instructions and, as soon as she did, the words "I LOVE YOU SARAH BARBER!" scrolled endlessly, line after line, down the screen.

"Wow!" she said. "That's so sweet. My husband, the computer programmer!"

As the months passed, Edwin bought several books on BASIC programming and learned enough to write a reasonably sophisticated program to catalog his wine collection. He could search for any wine in his cellar — actually, a shelf in the kitchen closet that held twenty-four bottles — by name, by color, by varietal type, and by region. Miraculously, the program worked, and Edwin was very pleased with the results of his learning.

Around this same time, Edwin was hired to work at a different company. He had been working with Kate Lewiston, a headhunter in town, to get a better job at a better advertising agency. And maybe it was providence but, at his new agency job, Edwin was assigned to work on The Home Office software account, which consisted of three programs: Home Office Writer, a word processing program; Home Office Planner, a spreadsheet program; and Home Office Card File, a data storage program that could do everything Edwin's TX-1000 data-storage program for his wine collection could do and a whole bunch more. And the software could do it so much faster. Edwin had outgrown the TX-1000. He was ready for a real computer that used real software.

Edwin bought a computer magazine and searched through the pages. He was dazzled by the number of choices for an actual computer: one with a monitor, and a keyboard with spring-loaded keys, and a floppy disc drive for loading and saving files.

Of the available IBM PC clones — the IBM PC was way too expensive — Edwin liked the Leading Edge computer.

He based his choice of the Leading Edge computer primarily on its cool red, white, and blue triangular logo, which, because Edwin was a design professional, appealed to him. The only drawback was the price, almost seventeen hundred dollars, cheaper than the computer hawked by the Chaplinesque "Little Tramp" in the TV ads, but expensive, nonetheless.

Edwin talked to Sarah, who also worked in advertising but at a different agency and in a more senior-level position. Sarah, who was the real money earner in the family, said they could afford the computer, but Sarah asked if they could wait a few weeks before making the purchase. She had a few large bills that had to be paid first. Edwin reluctantly agreed.

———

Two weeks passed, and it was Edwin's thirtieth birthday. His birthday that year occurred on a Tuesday, which meant he still had to get up, grab some breakfast, and carpool with Sarah to their respective jobs.

When he walked out of the bedroom, there on the dining room table was a fully assembled Leading Edge Model D computer with a floppy disc drive, a box of five-and-one-quarter-inch floppy discs, and a real live keyboard. The monitor had a black screen and amber colored text and displayed the Leading Edge nested triangles logo. Edwin was stunned. He was thrilled. He was ecstatic. He was so glad that he had had the good sense to marry Sarah Smithson, the woman of his dreams.

Sarah did her best impression of Vanna White from the "Wheel of Fortune" TV show and pointed with both hands to the computer. "Ta Da!" she crooned.

Edwin had never used a real computer before and was a little intimidated. But Sarah, who had read the instruction booklet fully and had assembled the computer in the dark of night, while Edwin was sound asleep, said, "Type in your name and then type in your password."

"Do I have a password?" Edwin asked.

"Your temporary password is MYCOMPUTER," Sarah said. "Type that in and then press the Enter key. It's the same idea as your Timex-Sinclair computer, Eddie."

And, so, Edwin, by using the real keyboard with the real keys that clicked when he pressed them, typed in his name, Edwin Barber, and then when prompted, he added his password, MYCOMPUTER, and tapped the Enter key with a flourish worthy of Liberace.

And scrolling endlessly down the screen was: I love you too Edwin Barber!!! I love you too Edwin Barber!!!

Who could have known that Sarah Barber was a computer programmer too?

The Reader

FOR DECADES, Roger had been reading books out loud twice a day to his wife, Elinor. These times were cherished moments in every day. Holidays included. Roger would read fiction in the morning with a cup of coffee and non-fiction in the evening with a glass of wine before dinner. There was no reason why Elinor did not do the reading aloud, herself — she wasn't ill, she was perfectly able to read, herself — in fact, she loved to read — the job of reader just seemed a better fit for Roger.

Elinor and Roger had a small library in their home with well over a thousand books, which they had read singly or together. The library contained books of fiction and non-fiction as well as a large collection of art books; books on philosophy; books on religion; even an entire set of the Oxford English Dictionary, which Elinor had inherited from her great aunt. There was an oeuvre of Oliver Sacks's books about how our brains work and large groupings of books by authors they both loved and enjoyed.

Interspersed among the books were framed photographs documenting the couple over the many years they had been married, which Roger liked to say was almost as many years as the number of books in their library. But let's skip back a few decades and discover how this tradition of reading books aloud came to be.

In the eighties, Elinor and Roger had a graphic design business in SOMA, the South of Market Area in San Francisco, and they commuted together from their home at the very north end of Marin County to their office in the city. At the end of the day, they retraced their route home, a commute of approximately seventy minutes in each direction.

They listened to NPR's, "Morning Edition" on the trip in and "All Things Considered" on the trip home. And this routine kept Elinor and Roger up to date and helped to pass the time on the lengthy commute. Before going to bed at night, they watched an hour of local news. Needless to say, they were well informed.

But, at this time in the eighties, there was tremendous unrest in the world: military conflicts, famine, flooding, and drought. And events closer to home were no more restful. The local news was dominated by stories about the homeless, shootings, road rage, carjackings, kidnapped children, plus a union-busting president who said one thing but did precisely the opposite to the benefit of the very wealthy and to the disadvantage of everyone else. Being sixties liberals, Elinor and Roger found all these events all the more painful to listen to and to watch.

The sheer volume of senseless violence, disorder, chaos, and the climate of division and hate was overwhelming. And this dreadful news continued non-stop from sunrise to bedtime. It was debilitating. It was too much.

One day while driving into the city, Roger switched off the radio and said, "You know Eli, we didn't create any of this, and there is not a damn thing that you and I can do to make it better. The news is destroying us. For the sake of our sanity, we have to pull back." And pull back they did.

They cancelled their daily paper. They stopped listening to and watching the news. They declared a news blackout. "If anything important happens," Elinor said, "Someone will be sure to let us know."

They announced their news blackout to their friends, who received the news with mixed reactions. Eli and Roger said that they were going to focus on positive things, things they could do, and things in their lives over which they had some control. "As far as the news is concerned," Roger said, "The world is just going to have to take two salt tablets and drive on," an expression Roger picked up in his two years in the military.

"It's irresponsible," their friends said. "It's your civic duty to know what is going on!" One of their closest friends said, "You guys just cannot do this." But Elinor and Roger smiled and said, "Watch us!" And their news blackout continued.

While almost everyone they knew was aware of their self-imposed news blackout, their friends and business associates would, just as Elinor had predicted, bring the couple up to date, whether or not the couple wanted to hear— and they definitely did not want to hear — about what was happening in the news.

Elinor was an avid reader and had been reading all her life. Roger was not a reader. In fact, early in their relationship, Roger stupidly announced to Elinor that he did not like women who read. Elinor responded, "But, I read, Roger. I love to read. I read all the time!" Oops.

There were painful reasons behind Roger's dislike for reading and people who read. When he was young, Roger's mother never read to him, and so he grew up without the love of books or the love of reading. As a youngster, he had mild attention deficit disorder. Reading was not easy for him, and his mind tended to wander. In class, when called upon to read aloud, he often mispronounced large words, resulting in ridicule and teasing from his classmates. And then, of course, there was his unfortunate penchant for speaking before thinking.

Roger did like listening to stories on the radio. He fondly remembered listening as a child to dramas and mysteries, such as "The Whistler" and "The Lux Radio Theater." He liked hearing stories read; he just was not keen on reading.

Elinor had some friends who were enthusiastic about Books on Tape, and these audio books seemed like the perfect solution to fill the void left by the absence of news programs during the long commute. They were very similar to Roger's early radio dramas. Elinor curated the reading/listening list, and she and Roger quickly became addicted to listening to books. On tape.

They listened to a number of books by Ernest Hemingway and amused themselves by keeping a running tally on a notepad of the number of drinks and bottles of grappa Jake consumed in *The Sun Also Rises*. They listened mostly to fiction but occasionally to non-fiction as well. And while listening was not actually reading, Roger began to gain an appreciation for good writing. The way different authors said the same thing but in such different ways, how some writers clearly articulated some things and other writers merely implied them, leaving it up to the reader to fill in the blanks.

Sometimes when Elinor and Roger were driving home from work, they would be at such a critical point in a book that they would pass their turnoff on the freeway and drive up to Petaluma, about twenty miles away. Or they would get home and sit in the car in the garage listening to the end of the chapter. The whole experience was books as theater, and often it was hard to put the taped book down.

Some readers were better than others, and some really brought life to the characters. When Elinor and Roger rented a book on tape and discovered that one of their favorite readers was doing the reading for that particular book, it intensified their enjoyment. Some authors read their own books, which added a certain intimacy to the story. There was one reader, though, that the couple just could not stand to listen to, and if the first thing they heard was this reader's voice when they started a new book, the cassette went immediately back into the box, and the box was immediately mailed back to Books on Tape.

Over time, Roger and Elinor were lured back into the real world by one salacious scandal or another: Clarence Thomas's Supreme Court confirmation hearings; the Iran-Contra revelations; the O. J. Simpson murder trial; the Exxon Valdez oil spill in Alaska. It was almost impossible not to be drawn back in, but Elinor and Roger continued listening to Books on Tape, their reward each day for living in such terrible times.

———

Eventually, after fifteen years of running their own business, they decided to close up shop and retire. Without the long daily commute, they had no more need for Books on Tape and, reluctantly, they cancelled their subscription.

However, not listening to a book every day created a new void in their daily routine. They missed being read to. Tremendously.

Then one day, Roger said, "Hey, Eli. What if we read books aloud from our own library? It would be like 'Poor Man's Books on Tape.'" And there were so many books, all of them Elinor's, that they could choose from. So, they took turns reading. Roger one day, Elinor the next. It was all very equitable.

Except, Roger's childhood attention deficit syndrome had never totally gone away, and he would miss large sections of Eli's reading because his mind wandered off. But when he read aloud, he was forced to concentrate on the words and content that he was reading. Speaking the words out loud helped him understand more about what he was reading. And so, it was agreed that Roger would be the designated reader, and Elinor the designated listener.

After reading fiction books aloud in the morning for several months with their morning coffee, Elinor suggested they read non-fiction books in the evening with wine before dinner. And the pattern was set. Fiction with mugs of coffee in the morning and non-fiction, or sometimes a mystery, with glasses of wine before dinner. In this way, Roger's "Poor Man's Books on Tape" continued for many, many happy years.

There was a most unexpected gift from all Roger's years of reading books aloud: he began writing his own stories. Some people said he was actually pretty good at it. He even found a company that was interested in publishing his stories. His uncanny ability to put the right commas in all the wrong places and his confusion between "that'" and "which" gave his editor plenty to do. But in the end, some of the stories were not too bad, and he had something to do in his retirement.

Roger also volunteered his time one day a week to read to groups of school children. Many of the children had reading disabilities similar to his own. He hoped to infuse these young minds with the joys of reading in the same way

Elinor had instilled a love of books in him.

One evening, Roger and Elinor were enjoying a particularly lovely glass of Napa Valley Merlot while reading what both agreed was one of the best non-fiction books ever — about how trees in a forest communicate with each other and help one another survive. On finishing the final chapter, Roger closed the book, took off his reading glasses and set them down on the table next to the book. "What do you think, Eli?" he asked.

"What do I think, Rog?" Elinor said before taking a reflective sip of her Merlot. "I think I like men who read!"

Texting Is a Drag

"HOLY CRAP, BRENDA! How can she do that?" Ollie asked. He and Brenda were streaming a movie in which one of the characters, a hip twenty-something woman, was texting with her thumbs at about a thousand words per minute. "I can't even hold my phone and hit the keys with one thumb," he continued. "Young people today must have extra bones in their thumbs."

"And she didn't even make a mistake!" Brenda observed with disgust. "Or not so's I noticed."

Ollie — that is, Oliver Wentworth — and his wife, Brenda, were raised in the era of the rotary-dial telephone. They grew up with such phone numbers as Hillside 32620 or Crestridge 52666. No area codes. It was a time when calling a number a few miles away was a toll call and cost a lot more than a "local" call. And nobody ever called long distance, unless there was an emergency or a death in the family.

"I just don't understand how they can do that. Bren, can you text like that, with your thumbs?" Ollie asked.

"No way. I tried it once, and my phone dropped out of

my hands. Just luckily it fell onto the carpet and not the tile floor. There was one of the younger women at work who was like that," Brenda said. "She could text really fast. With her thumbs. But she couldn't write nearly that fast on her computer. She hit the Backspace key almost every other word. And even then, she made a ton of mistakes. But on her cellphone, she was a speed demon. I'm afraid our brains are just not hardwired the same way."

"Ain't that the truth?" Ollie replied. "I just jab away at the phone with one finger, and I still miss half the keys. I always seem to be hitting the character next to the one I meant to hit."

At that point, an out-of-control red sports car came screeching around the corner and down the street with flash cuts to an older couple stepping off the curb in the movie they were watching, and their discussion was over.

———

A few weeks later, Ollie noticed one of his friends at the "Guys Lunch" — a group of friends who got together once a month to have lunch — sliding his finger over the keyboard on his iPhone. "What're you doing there, Jack?" Ollie asked. "Oh, this?" Jack inquired. "This is how I text. It's called drag-texting. Or at least that's what I call it. I think you can do this on most cellphones," he added. "Instead of hitting and missing half the keys with my fat fingers, I just drag from one letter to the next, and most of the time my phone seems to know what I want to say and pops the correct word onto the screen. I learned how to do it from one of the fellows in the office. He calls it "texting for old farts," Jack added with a big grin.

"Hmm. Cool," was all Ollie could think to respond with. "I'll have to give it try next time Brenda texts me. Or Skye, our daughter. You remember her, don't you? Can't believe she's out of college and working as a paralegal in Cincinnati. Those two are about the only people I ever text with. I'm still mostly an email or telephone guy. Hey, do you remember when we used to use our phones for making phone calls?"

Back in the office and with some time to kill between meetings, Ollie picked up his iPhone and created a new text message with no recipient. Slowly dragging from one letter to the next, he dragged, "I thing I can dothis." Although he meant to drag "think," he did notice that think was one of the suggested words over the keys.

He tried again, "I think I can do this," and he tapped the space bar twice for a period. "Ah," he noticed, "for I, as in me, I have to drag over the i character and then select the uppercase I from the choices, instead of using the Shift key. Okay, I get it. I can do this. Pretty cool."

Ollie then added Brenda's name in the recipient box and drag-typed, "Hey, Bren. I discovered a new way to test. Oops, text. I'll show you when we get home."

"I can hardly wait," came the response accompanied by an emoji with rolling eyes.

Ollie continued to practice and found that the phone

appeared to know about 90 percent of the time what he wanted to write, even when he did not drag over all the letters. He could just think of a word as he dragged across the keyboard, and his phone seemed to intuit what Ollie wanted to say. Sometimes the correct word appeared on the screen even after just a few letters.

That night when Brenda came home from work and they were both settled in the living room with their glasses of wine, Ollie said, "So, Bren, check this out." And he picked his phone up off the coffee table and drag-typed "This is an example of the miracle of drug testing." "Oh, hell," he said. "That should have been 'drag-texting.'"

"So, show me how you did that Ollie."

And Ollie revealed the very simple technique. "You just drag from one letter to the next. Some words are easier than others, and sometimes it's just simpler to punch in the actual characters, say, for a word like 'exponentially,' for example."

"Not a word I need to worry about, Oliver," Brenda said laughing, "but I see what you mean." Brenda drag-texted, "What are we having for dinner, Ollie?"

"By Jove," Ollie said, "I think she's got it. Well done, Bren."

With the demonstration over, the couple could now get down to some "serious drinking" and talking about their day at work, which Ollie admitted was largely consumed with practicing his drag-texting technique.

Over the coming weeks, Ollie and Brenda practiced

their drag-texting and then began to have competitions to see who could drag-text the fastest with the fewest mistakes. "OK, Bren, 'The quick brown fox jumps over the lazy dog.'" And looking at his watch, Ollie said, "Three, two, one . . . GO!" Approximately fifteen seconds later, Brenda finished with "The quick board fox jumps over the last dog."

"Not too bad, hon. Only two errors. My turn."

And Brenda counted down, and Ollie wrote in about twenty seconds, "The quack broken fox jumps quickly over the lazy doing." "Hmm," Ollie said. "Seems like I need more practice."

They challenged each other with such sentences as "Pack my box with five-dozen liquor jugs"; "Jackdaws love my big sphinx of quartz"; "Wafting zephyrs quickly vexed Jumbo"; "Crazy Fredericka bought many very exquisite opal jewels"; "Amazingly few discotheques provide juke-boxes," and other sentences that contained all the letters in the alphabet that they found by doing an internet search in their phones' browsers.

A few weeks later, both Ollie and Brenda could drag-text the same sentence perfectly in just around ten seconds. They were getting good at this. And since both Ollie and Brenda were competitive, it was becoming a nightly contest while they enjoyed their glass or two of wine before dinner. The loser of the contest had to make dinner for the other or do the wash for the coming week. It was a challenge they both took to and enjoyed.

While they were at work at their separate jobs, they started drag-texting each other, at first just silly messages with each other's cellphones vibrating every three or four seconds as their messages shot back and forth. Then the messages started to become more suggestive.

They had been married for more than thirty years, and the suggestive texting by a couple of empty-nesters took on an exciting, new, erotic tone for them.

Brenda would text Ollie at work, "Hey, Oliver, whatcha' doin' after work? Want to meet up for a drink?" And Ollie would text back, "You bet. We can hook up!" And Brenda would text back, "Might have to be a quickie before my husband gets home from bowling," followed by a handful of smiling emojis. And whoever got home first just might leave a trail of clothes leading to the bedroom for the other one to follow or other such inventive invitations.

At parties, they would drag-text suggestive messages from across the room to one another. "Bren, meet me in the hall closet in five." Only to be embarrassed when they emerged from the hall closet with hair mussed and clothing disheveled, as they encountered their host and hostess saying good night to some of their guests. They were starting to act like teenagers. People were beginning to notice. And talk. But Ollie and Brenda didn't care. Their flirtatious texting was great fun.

Until it wasn't.

One day, Ollie actually spoke without the aid of his cellphone and said, "Remember when phones were just for making phone calls?" And Brenda sighed and said, "Yes, I was just thinking the same thing."

And Ollie continued, "When we actually communicated by . . . talking? I'm getting nostalgic for the old days before we had these devices that let us text, and play games, and check the weather and the markets, and play music, and stream videos, and . . . basically separate you and me from the real world. And from each other. When we used to actually look at each other and have a meaningful or not-so-meaningful conversation."

Then without a thought, both turned away and picked up their cellphones. Brenda drag-texted, "Texting is a total drag!!! To which Oliver responded, "Time to hit reboot!"

The Boy Who Stuttered

DAVID'S EARLIEST AND MAYBE HAPPIEST CHILDHOOD MEMORY was of seeing a soldier walking down his street carrying something with a big yellow ribbon. The year was 1945, and David was almost three years old. The soldier was tall and wearing a starched khaki uniform. In his hand, he held a bright red toy truck wrapped in a yellow ribbon: a present for David.

The soldier stopped in front of David's house. He bent down and swooped David up in his arms and exclaimed, "My goodness. How much you have grown! Here, I have brought something for you." And he set David down on the sidewalk and handed him the toy truck.

David's mother came out of the house, and she asked David to take the toy truck into the house to play. The soldier and David's mother got into the family car, which was parked at the curb. But they did not go anywhere. They just sat there for a very long time and talked. And then the soldier got out of the car and walked — not quite as tall — back down the street in the direction from which he had come.

That night, David's mother seemed nervous and upset. She paced back and forth in the living room and was abrupt with David all during dinner. "Davie," she said, "for crying out loud, will you finish your dinner and stop dawdling? And take that truck off the table. It is almost time for bed."

The soldier was David's father, who was also named David. David's mother had sent him a letter while he was stationed in Italy during World War II asking him for a divorce. David Senior had come home on a hardship leave in a last-ditch attempt to try to work things out. But her mind was made up, and when Adrienne Bradley made up her mind about something, it was final. But at least, David's father did try.

———

When David Senior returned home from the war, he moved in with his mother, who lived a few miles away from his wife's home. The judge who divorced Mr. and Mrs. Bradley gave Adrienne full custody of young David but said David Senior could have visitation rights and could see his son one weekend every month, as long as he kept current on his child support payments. The judge asked the two parents to work out an alternating holiday schedule. The judge also thanked David Senior for his service to his country.

In June of 1946, one year after David Senior returned from the war, he married Elena, a woman he had met while he was stationed in Italy, who was with the USO, and who, we must assume, was the reason for the divorce. But young David knew none of this. His father's new wife was introduced to him on one of his monthly weekend visits as his "Auntie Elena," and David never questioned who Auntie Elena was or why his father was living with her and not with his mother and him. David was still very young, and some of the things that adults did made no sense to him. David was basically a happy child, and he just accepted things as they came. He assumed that fathers were nice people whom you visited once a month.

Adrienne, of course, was well aware of "Auntie Elena" and never missed an opportunity to speak ill of her ex-husband's new wife or of her ex-husband, for that matter. David found his mother's criticism of his father confusing. He did not particularly like or dislike Auntie Elena; she was just there in his father's house, and she and his father seemed to like each other. Auntie Elena was just part of the package. And that was that. Elena was not fond of David or children in general, but she did her best to be friendly. And she always made young David's favorite meal: pancakes with margarine and maple syrup and both bacon and sausage links.

One day, a man David had never met came to live with David and his mother. After the war, housing was in short supply and lodgings were hard to come by, and people frequently took in lodgers. The man was older than his mother.

He was funny, and he said silly things that made David laugh. He seemed to get along with Adrienne very well. His name was Harry. He had his own room in the house, and when he was at home, he would join them at the table for meals. Harry and David's mother would sit and talk after dinner. David could hear them for a few minutes before he fell asleep. He was happy because his mother seemed happier now, and she laughed a lot in a girlish way, something he had not heard her do for a long time. And she was nicer to David as well.

Harry had a job in the city composing music for a popular radio program. He was gone from 9 a.m. to 5 p.m. and most of the day on Saturday, when he directed the orchestra that provided the music for the radio program. The time when Harry was gone was the happiest time because David got to spend time alone with his mother. And, to be honest, he preferred it when it was just his mother and him.

———

At six-and-a-half years old, David did not have much of a concept of biological parents. He knew Adrienne was his mother, and he loved her very much. And he knew he had a father but, unlike most of his friend's fathers, his father did not live at home. But David Senior was his father, and he loved him very much as well. Auntie Elena was okay. He really loved his grandmother, and she absolutely adored him and spoiled him rotten at every opportunity. And that was really all that he needed to know.

So, David was deeply confused when one day, out of the blue, Adrienne announced to him that he was getting a new father. In fact, Harry, their lodger, was going to be his new father. David was speechless. It was just more than his young mind could fathom.

When he saw his real father that weekend for his monthly visit, David casually bragged to his father and Auntie Elena that he was getting a new father. The look of shock, mixed with sadness, mixed with anger showed on his father's face. The look on Auntie Elena's face was more of an "I told you so."

His father was at a loss for words. Finally, he composed himself and said, "Davie, I am your father, and I will always be your father. And I love you very, very much." Auntie Elena added, "Getting a new father! That's the stupidest thing I ever heard. You already have a father, Davie. Barry, or Harry, or whatever his name is will be your step-father. My David is your real and only father. Do you understand?"

Tears started welling up in young David's eyes, and he stammered, "N-n-no. I d-d-don't under-st-stand." And he burst into tears.

———

Around this same time David started to have disturbing dreams of two men in a cave filled with water with one man trying to drown the other man. He always awoke from this recurring dream frightened and confused. And around this same time, David began to stutter. Only when he was older did the metaphor of the dream become clear: the two men were David's real father and his step-father engaged in a life and death struggle.

———

Adrienne's marriage to Harry lasted less than two years, but David's stuttering went on for pretty much the rest of his childhood. He was literally at a loss for words. Speechless. His mother, who never suspected and would never admit that her offhand comment about a new father might have been the cause of David's stuttering, took David to a speech thera- pist to try to determine why this happy and cheerful little boy was suddenly sullen and had started stuttering. The speech therapist worked with Davie for several months but only with minimal results. She counselled Davie to speak slowly, to try to think of what he wanted to say before he spoke. But none of her advice really helped. If anything, the therapy may have made his stuttering worse.

But David learned to quickly substitute a word if he felt he could not pronounce the word he wanted to say and, for the most part, in casual conversation, he could tap dance his way through a sentence and nobody was the wiser. As a result, his vocabulary, especially for synonyms, grew quite rapidly. And his mother was comforted by the fact that her son's stuttering seemed to be a phase that he had now gone through. Of course, she was wrong.

David was at his most vulnerable when called upon in class to read aloud from a book. He was forced to read every word just as it was written. It was painful to watch while his face grew red and he stuttered his way through the paragraph. In his fifth-grade class, each student would read a paragraph or two and then call upon another student to continue. Being called upon to read was a constant source of dread for young David.

David was a good-looking boy, and the girls in his class liked him. To show this affection they would call on him to read after they had read. What should have been a happy time in young David's life was not.

When David reached high school, he was given a choice of languages to study, and he picked Spanish. He was a good learner and soon had a very good vocabulary, and grasp of the language, and knowledge of how to conjugate the verbs, except, of course, when called upon by the teacher to read aloud. And then he would try to clown his way out of reading by pretending not to know where in the book they were. And while this ruse may have amused his classmates, Señora Williams, his teacher, was not amused, and David was lucky to get only a C-minus in the class. After one year, he reluctantly dropped Spanish.

David went on to City College after high school. One of the required classes David had to take was public speaking. This class promised to be his worst nightmare but, being glib, David found he could improvise and substitute words for words he knew would catch him out. And, actually, he found that he liked public speaking and was pretty darn good at it. His instructor felt so as well, and David received one of the rare B-pluses in his not-so-stellar academic career.

He also made a discovery that affected his life in a very positive way, just as much as the announcement that he was getting a new father had affected his life in such a negative way. The more prepared he was, the better and more convincing his speech was. Being prepared gave him confidence. And confidence helped him to overcome his stutter.

David took the rapid transit bus to City College. It was easier than driving around endlessly hoping to find an empty spot in the over-crowded student parking lot. While he waited alone for the early bus, he would walk up and down in front of the bus stop and prepare for class by reading from his prepared notes. Word-for-word. And the more he prepared, the more his confidence grew until, finally, on the last day of class, he read his prepared speech from notes with only one or two pauses, which actually seemed to emphasize the points he was trying to make. It was one of the best days of his life.

———

After David graduated from City College, he got a job with a small public relations company. One of his fellow workers was Bradley, a handsome, athletic young man. All the young women in the office and in the bars he and David frequented considered Bradley catnip. It was almost embarrassing. Bradley appeared to have all the confidence in the world, until one day in a client meeting, Bradley started stuttering. He was humiliated. David totally felt his pain.

After work that night, David took Bradley out for a beer and confessed that he too was a secret stutterer and that he was always afraid that what happened to Bradley could happen to him at any time. Talking about this common fear seemed to help both Bradley and David, and Bradley said that he really appreciated David's support. Eventually, Bradley recovered his confidence, and the whole embarrassing episode faded from everyone's mind. But he and David formed a bond that would last for many years to come.

While the happiest ending to this story would be to tell you David went on to become President of the United States — he did have tremendous admiration and empathy for a fellow stutterer and the forty-sixth President of the United States — the truth is, from time-to-time, David still fears that his old doubts and hesitancy will come back and make him unable to pronounce certain words, that his painful, long-ago memories will resurface and bring back his stuttering. Happily, this has not happened, but for now, David will just take life one day and one word at a time.

The Butler Did It

Dear Mr. A. C. Doyle:

Thank you for your submission to *East End Detective Gazette*. We regret to inform you that we cannot accept your story, "The Butler Did It."

While we applaud your innovative approach of naming the murderer in the title of the story, unfortunately, all there is left for the reader is a long and somewhat tedious explanation of the murder itself.

Please understand that our readers enjoy the challenge of collecting the clues and then using these clues to ascertain the identity of the killer before this information is revealed by the author. You have put the proverbial cart before the horse. Do you see what I mean?

And clever though it was of you to have the murderer be the butler, I'm afraid the aforementioned butler is always the first person our astute readers suspect.

I hope my comments have been helpful, and we look forward to any more submissions you might have.

Your partner in crime,

Morry Arty
Editor and Publisher
East End Detective Gazette

# # #

Dear Mr. A. C. Doyle:

Thank you for your submission. We love the idea of a murder taking place on a jet plane at thirty thousand feet, where the murderer leaps from the emergency exit followed in hot pursuit by your fearless detective. And both jumping without parachutes! That your detective, Chief Inspector Jameson, is terrified of heights is a splendid touch. The fascinating and revealing dialog Chief Inspector Jameson has with the killer as they fall to earth in which the killer reveals the story of his tragic and turbulent childhood while CI Jameson handcuffs and reads the murderer his rights is almost as astounding as the two of them landing safely in the municipal pool. And the murderer's actually saving Chief Inspector Jameson's life because swimming is something the chief inspector — a city boy — never learned to do is a delightful, unexpected twist.

I am sorry to say, however, we currently have three other detective stories involving airplanes — I don't suppose this innovative plot would work aboard a luxury ship? Please do keep us in mind for further story submissions. You never know when we might be able to drop one of your stories into our publication.

Chuck Lindberg
Submissions Editor
Modern Detective Magazine

# # #

Dear Mr. A. C. Dull:

We are delighted that you thought of us as potential publishers for your story "Murder at Sea." Regrettably, a detective, a murderer, and a victim in a lifeboat in the middle of the Indian Ocean seems a bit thin plot-wise. Traditionally, as you are well aware, a good "whodunit" has an assortment of suspects the reader must plow through looking for clues to determine who exactly the murderer is. Frequently, but not always, the butler. That sort of thing.

Your idea might be more appropriate if it took place on an overbooked airliner at thirty thousand feet, a Boeing 777-300ER filled with suspects, for example.

The editors did find it terribly inventive that your murderer used the emergency rations shrimp cocktail, which was well past its sell-by date, to poison his victim. But the lack of motive, and the sketchy character development left us clinging to the life jackets.

We have a sinking feeling that this lifeboat murder mystery will never make it to home port.

Do keep us in mind if you come up with another thriller.

Edward Smith
Chief Steward and Editor
Captain's Table Magazine

# # #

Dear Mr. A. C. Doll:

The editorial staff here at *Barn & Farm Almanac* were amused at your proposed submission of a detective story about a goat that solves crimes of passion assisted by his barnyard buddies. We applaud your imagination, but we must reject this story; its frivolous tone and manner are just not appropriate in these difficult financial times in the farming and livestock industry.

We wish you the best of luck and assure you that our rejection of your story has nothing to do with the quality of your writing, which is comparable to GMO corn.

Sincerely
William Pullet
Editor and Chief
Barn & Farm Almanac

#

Dear Mr. A. C. Doyle:

We are returning your submission. *The Poughkeepsie Psychic Review* does not publish detective stories. Although we can usually foresee what will arrive in the mail, your story, "I Murdered My Psychic, and She Never Saw It Coming," we must admit caught us completely off guard.

We would love to say we see a positive future for you in detective-fiction writing but, sadly, this positive future is just not in the cards as we see them now.

With one eye on the future and the other around the corner,

Madame Josephine Tarot
Publisher
The Poughkeepsie Psychic Review

#

Dear A. C. Doyle:

Reading your submission, "The Type-hound of the Baskervilles," brings to mind a memorable book with a similar title written by a brilliant author with a similar name. Your first and middle names would not happen to be Arthur Conan by any chance? Just a wild guess.

The idea of a famous type detective to whom advertising art directors and graphic designers bring fragments of headlines at his place of business on 221 Baker Street, Suite B, to track down the family name of the typeface, or font, as we in the industry call it, is a curious one. We must admit, it is a story angle we have never seen before. Why you have selected us as a potential publisher is something of a mystery but, I regret to say, not one in which our readers might engage. You see, our readers are design professionals and typographers, most of whom can identify a type family and font, if you will, by just seeing a question mark or an italic ampersand. Some of our readers can even tell a Garamond from a Baskerville or Bodoni simply from a period!

We do wish you best of luck with your writing. This submission is just not our type of story.

Bernard Schlepps
Director
Just Your Type Quarterly

# # #

Dear Ace Doyle:

We have read your submission, and we have concluded that ██████████ you must be confused about the nature of our business. I'll try to explain. At *Clandestine Leak Detection Journal,* we focus on ██████████ ██████████ ██████████ security breaches at the highest levels of business and ██████████ government. We publish articles that focus on stopping leaks of classified and sensitive information ██████████ before they become public.

Your story features a detective who searches out underground water leaks, and though we were amused that your detective carries a toilet plunger instead of a cane, this characterization, frankly, is just not the kind of leakage our readers expect.

I highly recommend you submit this story to the *Pipe Fitters Journal* or *Plumber's Digest*.

Securely Yours,
S. L. Loothe
Editor
Clandestine Leak Detection Journal

# # #

My Dear A. C. Dolle:

Let me begin by acknowledging receipt of your submission, "Walking Back Murder." What an utterly novel idea: a story in which everything happens backwards from the murder in the first paragraph. Your female detective, Ms. Cheryl Locke-Holmes, reenacts the entire murder as if in a film in which everything is played in reverse, with all the characters walking backwards, vehicles moving in reverse, and so forth.

Unfortunately, by page two, we were fatigued, and by page four of your twenty-three-page story, not one of our editorial review board members was still awake.

And so, although we applaud your backward approach to detective fiction, we regret we must reject your story.

But, please, do not give up. We encourage you to submit more stories and look forward to seeing what other inventive ideas you have.

Yours truly,

Earle Strange
Publisher and Editor-In-Chief
Walks and Rocks

# # #

Dear Mr. A. C. Doyle:

We are pleased to announce our intention to publish your submission, "A Study in Scarlet, the Adventures of Sherlock Homes." We have a few tiny changes that we think will make this incredible tale a much more engaging read.

Sherlock Holmes is an interesting name, but we are concerned it might not appeal to our younger readers. It sounds a bit old-fashioned and fussy, a name more appropriate for a dealer in used motor vehicles. We asked our editorial staff for some suggestions, and the name we all agreed on was Jack Jones; the alliterative J has a very manly ring.

We conducted a "mother-in-law survey," which is to say, we asked some of the secretaries in the office whether they knew what color scarlet is, and what we discovered is that most of them associated scarlet not with a color but with the heroine in *Gone With the Wind!* We feel strongly that something along the lines of red or brown might be more palatable. "A Study in Beige" has a nice ring to it, wouldn't you agree?

And — one just has to ask — does anyone actually wear a deer stalker hat and cape? Exotic though you think this outfit might be, our panel strongly suggests something more *au courant*: jeans and a dark T-shirt (or perhaps a color that matches the color in your title).

Your narrator and confidant, Dr. Watson, we feel, just begs to be more aggressive. Doctors, we fear, might be too soft to engage our readers. Furthermore, most people are afraid of doctors. And let's face it, a doctor as a narrator? Nobody listens to doctors! What would you think if Watson were a football coach? Or maybe a stockbroker? Or a biker? We welcome your suggestions.

We hate to harp, because we absolutely love this mystery but, that said, while the violin requires a high degree of skill and might help Jack Jones when he is pondering the great imponderables, we all agree that something along the lines of an electronic keyboard or an electric guitar will work just as well and will resonate better with our readers.

One last suggestion that we all feel will draw in our younger readers: instead of the pipe — too professorial — how about a vape pen?

If these tiny, tiny changes are acceptable, please submit your revised manuscript at your earliest convenience.

Ward Lock
Editor
Lippincott's Magazine

P.S. I almost forgot to mention: one of our junior editors had a brilliant plot twist that we strongly urge you to consider. Instead of Mr. Hope's being the murderer and your readers having to traipse all over two continents through what is unarguably a plot laden with impossible-to-follow twists and turns, how about we just have the butler commit the murder? Surely no one would *ever* suspect the butler! Brilliant, no?

— AFTERWORD —

This is my second book of fiction. I want to thank you who, for whatever reason, purchased this book. And especially any of you who have read this far. I hope you enjoyed the stories and are still awake.

Heartfelt thanks to Allison Smith for her patience and invaluable help and incredible editing skills. Without your assistance I never would have been able to get my nouns and verbs, let alone Ernest's watch and cell phone, to agree.

Thanks and giant hugs to Mary Carter, my wife and the real writer in the family who patiently listened while I read each story aloud and then generously offered solutions and suggestions that made these stories better.

Lifelong gratitude to Art Center College of Design for giving me the skills to earn a living in advertising and an eye for type design that I put to use in designing this book.

And if I do not thank Sophie and Chloe, our most excellent calico cats, I will never hear the end of it.

– ABOUT THE AUTHOR –

Gary W. Priester graduated from the Art Center College of Design and worked for fifteen years as an advertising art director in Los Angeles, and San Francisco.

For twelve years, Priester and his wife Mary Carter ran The Black Point Group, a graphic design company located in the SOMA district of San Francisco.

For over two decades Priester and Gene Levine have created hidden image 3D stereograms for publication and for advertising and graphic design companies.

Gary W. Priester lives in Placitas, New Mexico with his wife, author Mary Carter and their two cats: Chloe and Sophie. Carter and Priester divide their time between Placitas and Bernalillo.